Praise for Close to the Wind

'I can't recommend it highly enough . . . Walter has created something very special with Close to the Wind.' Philip Ardagh, Guardian

'A beautiful read.' '[An] original and cleverly plotted tale of betrayal, sacrifice and ingenuity.'

The Sun

'A g   Children's
mo   Book of the Week
be missed.'   Independent on Sunday

'An   the most human level.
It has the fable-like quality   Hartnett and I read it
at one sitting.' The Bookseller

'Th Silver Sword-   Tory is a feel-good book.'
Jewish Chronicle

'A brilliant, well-written debut novel.'

whi   g
it is to believe in something
as strongly as often only   Wondrous Reads Blog
a chil   'A beautiful and heart-breaking
Viva   will not be able
                             ry eyed.'

'A superbly   owing
Surrey Advert   Blog

CLOSE
TO THE
WIND

JON WALTER

David Fickling Books

31 Beaumont Street
Oxford OX1 2NP, UK

Close to the Wind
is a
DAVID FICKLING BOOK

First published in Great Britain by
David Fickling Books,
31 Beaumont Street,
Oxford, OX1 2NP

Hardback edition published 2014
This edition published 2015

978-1-910200-17-9

1 3 5 7 9 10 8 6 4 2

David Fickling Books supports the Forest Stewardship Council (FSC), the
leading international forest certification organization. All our titles that are printed
on Greenpeace-approved FSC-certified paper carry the FSC logo.

DAVID FICKLING BOOKS Reg. No. 8340307

A CIP catalogue record for this book is available from the British Library

Printed and bound in Great Britain by Clays Ltd, St Ives plc

To my wife Tanya – for everything

Part 1

The boy and the old man arrived at the port at night.

There had been cloud in the sky but now the moon shone brightly and they stood in the shadow cast by a row of terraced cottages that lined a cobbled street, polished through the years by wheels and feet and the hooves of horses.

The boy held the old man's hand.

The air smelled of motor oil and charred timber. At the far end of the street, the quayside was lit by a bright white lamp that glared upon the skeleton of a single black crane, its hook hanging solemn above the cottage roofs, and above the crane loomed the tall ship, a string of yellow bulbs along the rails of its upper decks as though it might be Christmas and not a warm autumn night.

The boy sneezed loudly.

'Shhh, Malik,' hissed his grandfather.

Malik let go of his grandfather's hand and pinched his nose through the white cotton handkerchief that covered his face – his grandfather had tied it across his nose and mouth to protect him from smoke. Malik could have removed the cloth, since they were a long way from the fires, but he kept it, believing it made him look older. He held his breath so that he wouldn't sneeze again. When he was certain, he took his hand away. 'Sorry, Papa.'

Papa settled a hand on Malik's shoulder. 'No. I'm sorry. I didn't mean to bite.' He glanced back down the road behind them. 'I'm still nervous. I'm sure there's no one here, but we ought to be careful.'

'Careful as a cat,' said Malik.

'Fearful like a fox,' said Papa, and he adjusted the rucksack that he carried slung from a single shoulder.

Malik nodded. He felt sorry for the foxes – nobody ever had a good word to say about them. He saw Papa's eyes flick to either end of the street and his stomach tensed as though he were about to be punched. These moments of uncertainty were the worst. He put a hand to the front of his trousers and held himself.

Papa looked down at him. 'Do you need the toilet?' Malik shook his head. 'Then don't do that, eh? You're too old for that.'

Malik put his hand in his trouser pocket. He shuffled on his feet, stepping from one side to the other so that the tops of his green Wellington boots flapped against his trousers. Papa's eyes went up and down the row of cottages; he was checking for something.

Malik stopped shuffling and lifted himself on tiptoes so as to be closer to Papa's ear. 'Is that our ship?'

Papa pulled the collar of his thick winter coat away from the back of his neck. His brow was damp with sweat. 'I expect it is,' he said quietly. 'I can't see the name, but it's the only ship here.'

Malik looked again and he agreed. There were no other ships.

Papa put a hand to his short, white beard and tugged at the hair, something he did when he was thinking. 'We're too early. We can't go there yet. I think we must wait till the morning.'

The muscles in Malik's stomach twisted – Papa would need to find them a place to stay again. Last night they had slept in the basement cellar of a burnt-out office block and there had been a dying dog. He followed Papa's eyes to the row of cottages, silhouetted in the bright light from the quay, the chimneys standing proud of the grey slate roofs. If they couldn't go to the ship, then perhaps they could spend the night in one of these. Malik hoped so. He imagined a chair to sit in. A basin for washing. His own bed.

'Will the ship leave tomorrow?'

Papa ignored the question and Malik felt guilty

for having asked it, but he had other questions, all sorts of questions, and he couldn't help himself.

'Is this where we're staying?' he asked. 'Is this where Mama will meet us?'

Papa raised his voice. 'So many questions. I've told you about that. How many questions is that you've asked today?'

Malik dropped his head. 'I don't know.'

'You don't know? Well, I don't know either. There's been so many I've lost count. But we agreed on ten, didn't we? We had an agreement and we shook hands on it. Only ten questions each day.' Papa took a deep breath and lowered his voice. 'I reckon you've got just one left and that's being generous. You should be careful – think about what you say before you open your mouth.'

Malik tightened his jaw. Papa never liked too many questions: he had learned that in the last two days. He stepped again from one foot to the other, thinking of what he could get away with saying next. A question mark hung over everything. 'How do you . . . I mean . . . what should I . . . ?' He reached for Papa's hand, gripped his index finger. 'It's impossible.'

'No. It's not impossible. It's difficult, I'll grant you

that.' Papa squeezed Malik's fingers then knelt beside him and pointed. 'See that cottage there? The one with the dark red door?'

Malik was disappointed. 'The one with the broken window?'

'Yes. That's the one. I want you to count the houses from this end of the street till you get to the one with the broken window. Tell me how many houses there are before you reach the one we want.'

This was one of Papa's games. Malik knew them now, the little things Papa gave him to do to keep his mind occupied. It was what Mama used to do when he was young but Malik didn't mind Papa doing it now. It was better than having too much time to think.

He began to count under his breath, nodding his head at each house. 'Thirteen,' he said.

'Are you sure?' Papa narrowed his eyes. 'I made it twelve. Let's do it together.'

They began to count and Papa pointed at each cottage in turn. Malik took hold of his hand to stop him after seven. 'No, Papa. Look. That one's different. That's two houses. There's another front door. See? A shared porch with two front doors.'

Papa's eyes flicked to the walls either side of the

porch. He checked the windows. 'Yes, I see. You're right. One porch but with two front doors. Two eyes are better than one, eh?' He touched the top of Malik's head. 'We make a good team.'

Malik's mouth whipped up into a smile. 'Who lives there? How do we know them? Are they friends of ours?'

Papa didn't seem to mind the questions. He checked the street again to make sure they were safe. 'I hope no one lives there. They should have left when the trouble started. I don't think anyone still lives in these streets.'

A cloud moved across the moon and the cobbles on the street turned black. An engine started up from somewhere in the distance, probably from the quayside.

Papa took hold of Malik's hand. 'I think we should go.'

'Is it soldiers?'

'I don't think so. But we've been here too long. We should be out of sight. Come on.'

Papa stepped out across the street and Malik ran to keep up, his head ducked low to avoid the rucksack which bounced from side to side on Papa's back. They hurried to the opposite pavement, rounded the final cottage and slipped into the alley that divided the back of the houses in this street from the next.

Papa stopped running and drew Malik close to him by the hand. 'It's very dark, isn't it? Now the moon has gone, I can't see my own feet.'

Malik looked for his own feet and saw nothing but black. He held a hand up to his face, moved it toward his nose and away again.

'We'll go slowly,' Papa whispered. 'Count the houses for me, will you? We want number thirteen.'

'I can't see the houses, Papa. It's too dark.'

Papa put an arm round Malik's shoulder. 'You're right. It's too dark to see the houses.' He lifted Malik's hand and his fingers brushed against brickwork. 'Feel that, Malik? That's the back wall to the yard of the first house. We can count the gates till we reach thirteen.'

They walked into the darkness, holding hands. 'It's too dark,' Malik complained. 'I don't like the dark.'

'No,' agreed Papa. 'Nobody likes the dark. But you should remember that there's no one here and the dark can't hurt us.'

Malik knew that Papa couldn't really know that for certain – you can never know for sure if there's anything in the dark. 'Can we use the torch?'

'No. We don't need the torch.'

'I do.'

'No, you don't. Feel with your fingers.'

'It would be better with the torch.'

'Malik! We can't use the torch. They could see the torch.' Papa caught his breath and stopped walking.

Malik came up close against him. He tried to see Papa's face. 'You said there were no soldiers. You told me it was only us. If there's no one here then no one can see the light.'

'Yes.' Papa sighed. 'I suppose you're right.' He took the rucksack from his back and placed it on the floor. 'You're using logic and I can't argue with that. I suppose we don't need to whisper either.'

'The torch is in the top pocket, Papa. The one on top of the flap that goes over.'

'Yes. Thank you. I remember.' Papa slid back the zip and took out the thin metal torch, twisting the bulb casing till the light came on and turned the edge of his fingers pink.

'Can I hold it?'

Papa put the torch into Malik's hand and directed it down to the floor. 'Keep it pointed at the ground.

Just down near your feet.' The thin beam picked out the green rubber of Malik's Wellington boots. 'Your feet must be hot in those boots. You'll be able to take them off soon.'

'I don't mind.' Malik nudged the torch beam ahead of his feet and the shaft of light showed a little yellow flower, sprouting up between the broken stones that paved the alley. 'Look. I nearly trod on a flower.'

'It's a weed, Malik. A dandelion.'

Malik stooped and broke the stem of the yellow flower. 'It's for Mama,' he said. 'I'm going to save it for her.'

They went on through the darkness, but quicker now they had some light. They counted the gates as they passed. The torch picked out one that was painted red and another that was green. At the thirteenth gate, an upturned metal bin lay on the ground with rubbish spilling from the open top. Something smelled rotten. The torch showed them an open can lying on its side, used teabags and half a cauliflower that was almost black. Malik stepped on a soiled newspaper. Above him the clouds thinned enough to give them a little light. This was the thirteenth house.

'Is this it?' Malik's breath moved the handkerchief on his face. He flicked the torch up to Papa's face and saw him turn and scowl.

'Yes, this is it. Put the torch out now, will you? The moon will give us enough light.'

Malik turned off the torch and they paused. Papa put his hand into the pocket of his coat and Malik knew that in Papa's pocket there were two red apples and the knife with the blade that folded back into the curved wooden handle. He had seen Papa reach into his pocket and touch it before, always when he needed courage. Malik wanted a knife just like that.

Papa took two steps to the gate, twisted the metal latch and opened it. The moonlight showed them the back of the cottage through the open gate. Malik could see a back door with pretty glass squares, and to the right of it a window. It looked like a nice house. Small, but comfortable.

Papa tugged at his beard. 'You better stay here.'

'Why? I don't want to.'

'It's better for you to wait while I check to see that it's all right.'

'To see if there's a dead dog?'

'No. Not to see if there's a dead dog. There won't be another dead dog, Malik.'

'How do you know?'

Papa put a hand to his head and closed his eyes. 'No. No, that's too many questions. You're doing it again.' He held out his hand and sliced the air into sections as he spoke. 'I don't know for certain. Of course I don't. But it's unlikely. It's very unlikely. It would be unfortunate to find another dead dog.'

Malik gripped the little yellow flower in his hand and remembered the dead dog on the cellar floor, down by the metal grille. It hadn't been dead at first but it was now. It was probably still on its own, lying where they had left it.

'Please, Papa. I don't want to wait here on my own.' Malik tried not to whine, and hoped Papa wouldn't be angry.

Papa nodded. 'OK.' He took hold of Malik's hand. 'Let's go together.'

They stepped across the yard and found the back door locked. Papa went to the window, put his face against the glass, then came back to Malik. 'I need the handkerchief from your face.' He reached around, undid the knot at the back of Malik's head, then wrapped his hand in the cloth and punched through one of the small panes, just above the doorknob. The sound of breaking glass shattered the silence. Malik held his breath, half expecting a shout or a rush of feet, but nothing happened.

Papa unwound the handkerchief from his fingers. He had a single small cut on the middle knuckle and he put it to his mouth, sucked away the blood, then reached inside and turned the key that was in the lock. The hinges of the door creaked as he opened it and stepped inside. He looked back at Malik. 'You'd better turn the torch on.'

Malik twisted the top of the torch and followed Papa. The beam picked out wallpaper the colour of cornflowers, and that looked very pretty, but it was only the top half of the wall. The bottom half had bare plaster with corrugated ridges of brown glue where the kitchen units had been pulled away. Two pipes ran along the skirting board and had been capped off with a simple tap where there had once been a sink. On the floor, below the tap, stood a yellow plastic bucket full of discarded drink cans. Malik trod on screws and broken bits of masonry as he turned the torch around the empty room. He should have known it would be like this.

'It might be better through here.' Papa stepped onto the bare floorboards of the dark hall. 'Come on, hand me the torch.'

They crept along the passage till the beam picked out a door. Papa pushed it open and stepped inside the hollow room. There was no furniture and no carpet. A ragged hole in the brickwork of the opposite wall showed where the fireplace had once been, and no curtain hung across the broken glass of the window. There was no comfort to be found here. None at all.

'There's nothing here, Papa.'

'No, Malik. I can see. People have been here. They've stripped the house bare. Everything that was worth anything has gone. You can be certain of that.'

Malik walked over to the window and looked out across the empty street. This was only just better than the cellar. Mama wouldn't like this house at all, and she wouldn't want to come here.

Malik stood with Papa at the foot of the staircase. He should have known, the moment they'd sneaked in through the back, that this house would be no good.

There had been a time when Malik used only front doors. He would ring the bells or give two raps on the knocker and his friends would come outside or they would invite him in. Everyone he knew had nice houses, not all of them as large as his, but always pleasant in one way or another and there would be food and drink and games to play.

He stared at the front door of the cottage. It had two panels of frosted glass that were dark with the night. A single brown envelope hung from the inside of the letterbox, halfway up the door, sticking part in, part out. Papa reached out and pulled it free. He put the torch close to the paper, read the name on the envelope and then opened it. Malik saw writing in red ink.

'Final notice from six weeks ago,' said Papa. 'They must have left the house before it arrived.'

They climbed the stairs, Papa out in front and Malik following behind, his Wellington boots squeaking on the wooden staircase. At the top of the stairs was a bathroom that had the fittings removed. The outline of the bath and sink could be traced from the tiles that finished halfway up the wall and the toilet was nothing but a sluice pipe that sat up ten centimetres from the floor.

They pushed another door and found a bedroom. This room at least had furniture. A white painted wardrobe was at the other end to the door and there was a single wooden chair and a bare mattress on the floor. The window had a thick blue curtain drawn back to one side. Balanced on the windowsill was an ashtray brimming with the crushed tips of thin cigarettes that had been rolled by hand.

Papa looked inside the wardrobe. He let the rucksack drop to the floor beside the mattress and shone the torch back to the doorway where Malik stood. 'We have a mattress. At least it's something. It's better than last night.'

Malik shrugged.

Papa said, 'Who's going to have it? You or me?'

'Mama should have it.' Malik hesitated, but he asked the question anyway. 'When will she be here?'

The questions about Mama always annoyed Papa the most, but Papa answered him gently. 'Not tonight, Malik. I said she would meet us when the ship sailed, and that's not till tomorrow. We'll see her at the dock when we go there tomorrow. I'm sure we will.'

Malik's head dropped. He saw the dandelion in his fist and he held it up. 'What shall I do with this?'

Papa took the dandelion from his hand. 'Let's go and see whether we have any water.'

They went downstairs to the kitchen. Papa turned

the metal tap on the bare pipe and it shuddered and spat and ran with water. He took a drinks can from the bucket, pulled the ends to straighten it out and filled it with water, then he dropped the stalk into the can so that the yellow head rested on the silver rim and he put the can onto the windowsill where he said it would get the morning sun.

Papa touched Malik's shoulder. 'Now let's see if we can get some rest.'

They went back into the hallway and the beam of the torch picked out chipped paintwork on the bannister. They climbed the stairs to the bedroom and Malik sat down on the mattress while Papa pulled the curtain across the window. 'It's thick enough to shield the light,' Papa said, more to himself than to Malik. 'I'll light us a candle. Let's see if we can make this place more comfortable.' He took off his coat and hung it on the back of the wooden chair.

Malik put the torch on the floor and picked at a loose end of cotton ticking while Papa retrieved the rucksack from beside the wardrobe and put it down in the beam of light that spread out across the floorboards.

'What's the matter with you?' he asked Malik.

'Nothing.'

Papa removed a pair of blue denim trousers and a white shirt from the sack and laid them on the floor. He brought out a pair of socks, some shorts and a warm brown jumper. 'Do you want this on?'

Malik shook his head and Papa placed the jumper on the pile of clothes.

Papa then found a box of six wax candles with one already used. 'Here we are,' he said. He slid one of the white candles from the box, opened the lid of the brass zippo that he took from his trouser pocket and lit the wick. He turned the candle upside down so that the wax dripped onto the floorboard before he stood the candle upright. 'Better turn the torch off,' he told Malik. 'It will save the battery.'

Malik left the torch alone. He twisted the loose piece of material round his finger instead, let it go, then twisted again.

Papa reached across and switched the torch off himself. The light in the room became faint and yellow and it flickered. 'Why don't you tell me what the matter is?'

Malik wouldn't answer him.

It had been two days since the soldiers had come to the house and his mother had hidden him in the wardrobe. She had told him not to move, told him not to make a sound, and Malik had waited and waited. He hadn't said a word. Even when he'd thought he'd heard Papa's voice, he hadn't called out.

'Do you want to see my magic trick?'

Malik shook his head.

Papa put the clothes back into the main body of the sack, then he opened one of the large side pockets. He brought out a ball of thick yellow twine, a hammer, a screwdriver and a pair of pliers, which he lined up along the floorboard behind the candle. He looked over at Malik. 'Well, there must be something I can do to cheer you up.'

Malik showed a flicker of interest as his eyes glanced up to Papa's face. 'Can I have a knife?'

'You don't need to think about knives.'

'You've got one. I've seen it. You keep it in your jacket pocket.'

'Yes I do.'

'I saw you holding it last night when we went to sleep in the cellar. Was that because of the dog?'

'No. Of course it wasn't because of the dog. The dog was half dead, he wasn't going to hurt us.'

'I know.'

Papa held up his hands in a gesture of defeat. 'Oh, good grief.' He stood up and fetched the key ring from his jacket pocket, unfastened a penknife that was the length of his smallest finger and handed it to Malik. 'Be careful of the blade. It might be small but it's very sharp. And I don't want you to lose it. I had that knife for my tenth birthday. It was the only thing I asked for and my father bought it for me.'

Malik put his fingernail to the main blade and pulled it out from the handle.

Papa watched him. 'Perhaps I'll give one to you as a present when you're ten.'

'I'm already ten.'

'Never. Are you sure?'

Malik looked at him with disgust. 'Of course I'm sure. It was my last birthday.'

'Was it? And I didn't give you a knife?'

'No. You gave me a geometry set.'

'With a wooden and brass compass?'

The boy nodded and Papa thought about it. 'Well, I've got them the wrong way round. Why would I do that? You should have a Swiss army knife when you are ten and a geometry set when you are eleven. That's what I was given as a boy. I wonder what I was thinking?' The old man looked confused. 'What did I get for your ninth birthday?'

'I can't remember.'

'No. Nor can I. It's all too long ago.'

They paused.

'Mama would know. She can tell us tomorrow.'

Papa pressed his forehead with the tips of his fingers but he nodded. 'Yes, yes. I expect she will.' He began to search through the rucksack again. He took out a toothbrush and toothpaste and waved them in Malik's face. 'You should do your teeth.' He found the red steel water bottle from the rucksack. 'Come on, come to the bathroom.' He got to his feet slowly, his hand on the small of his back. 'And bring the torch with you.'

Malik shone the beam down the broken end of the pipe where the toilet had been but could see no water. Papa got on his hands and knees to inspect it further. 'It will be OK. It doesn't smell and it must still lead into the sewers. We can use that.' He got to his feet so slowly that Malik expected his knees to creak. Papa straightened up, nodded at Malik and then at the pipe. 'You will need to pee.'

Malik looked into the deep black hole. 'I'm not using that. I don't like it.'

'I'm sure you don't but we don't have a choice. You can pee standing up if your aim is good – and you don't have to flush. That's one less thing to think about.'

Papa went back into the bedroom and Malik pushed the door till it was almost closed. He leaned the torch against the wall to give him light and then he sluiced his mouth with water from the bottle and swallowed it. He scrubbed his teeth and spat the white foam down the hole.

Papa had brought the toothpaste that Malik liked. It wasn't the one Mama used – that tasted of aniseed. Papa had brought the minty one that was Malik's. He had remembered his toothbrush too. So this must have been planned, just like Papa said it was. And that meant Mama would be at the dock tomorrow.

The thought cheered Malik up, though not enough that he was going to have a pee. He looked at the pipe sticking up from the floor. If he waited till the morning he would find somewhere better.

Papa was packing the tools back into the ruck-sack when Malik jumped onto the mattress.

'Hey. None of that.' Papa waved a hand in his direction. 'Come on. It's time for sleep. You must be shattered.'

'I'm not.'

'You must be tired. You walked twice as far as I did.'

'I walked the same as you.'

'The same distance, yes, I'll grant you. But your legs are only half the length, so you had to make twice as many strides as me.' Papa felt the back of his thighs. 'If I'm tired, you must be too.'

Malik jumped again. 'Well, I'm not tired. My legs are fine.'

Papa frowned. 'In that case you better let me have the bed. Anyway, it should be mine by rights, since I'm the one who aches. I probably have brittle bones.'

Malik stopped jumping and stepped quickly off the mattress. 'You can have the bed, Papa. I don't mind.'

Papa stood up from his chair. He sucked at his teeth, put his hands on his hips, thought about it, then sat back down. 'No. You better have it. It wouldn't be right. I was simply saying you should appreciate it. That's all. You shouldn't take it for granted. Now, be a good boy and take off your boots.'

Malik slipped off the green Wellington boots, picked them up and stood them against the skirting board by the door.

'Are you too hot to sleep in your clothes?'

Malik shook his head.

'Then you must lie down and go to sleep.'

'You said you would show me your trick again.'

'So you want to see it now?' The old man heaved himself up again with a sigh. 'OK. I will do it for you, but only the once.' Papa took a coin from his pocket. He held it on the open palm of his hand, right in front of Malik's eyes. 'What do we call this trick?'

'The French Drop,' said Malik.

'Exactly. The French Drop. Good. You take an everyday coin and . . .' Papa yawned and stretched out the sentence. He closed one hand with the fingers of his other and put the hand holding the coin to his mouth. When he opened it the coin was gone.

Papa let his jaw drop wide so Malik could see his big pink tongue. 'It's not in my mouth.' He leaned towards Malik, took the coin from behind Malik's ear and held it up in front of his face. He grinned. 'Did you see that? Do you remember how it's done? You can't have forgotten already?'

Malik stood up and held his hand out for the coin. Papa gave it to him and sat back down in the chair, waiting to be entertained. 'Remember, sleight of hand. A larger action covers a smaller action. That's why I did the big yawn.'

Malik had tried the trick before and he always dropped the coin. He couldn't hide it in the palm of his hand like Papa did – he didn't think his thumb was the right size. He held the coin up to show it to Papa, then closed his fingers across the top with his other hand. He coughed, putting one hand to his mouth while the hand with the coin darted down the front of his trousers.

Papa scoffed and slapped his thighs. 'What are you doing?'

Malik showed him an empty palm as though he had got away with it.

Papa shook his head and smiled. 'How will you make it reappear if it's down your pants?'

'I'm concentrating on the disappearance.'

'I can see that. But I'm not going to be happy if I don't get my coin back. Mind you, I'm not sure I want it back now I know where it's been. Why not practise hiding it like I do? It's easier to hide it in your palm. See?' Papa took another coin from his pocket and held it in his palm using only his thumb, to show him how it was done.

Malik shook his head. 'It's too difficult. I can't do it. It's easier in my pants.'

'But I saw where you put it. Trust me, it's easier in your hand. It just takes practice, lots of practice, until you get it perfect.'

Malik put his hand into his underpants, retrieved the coin and gave it back to Papa, who turned the coin once in his fingers before putting them both back in his pocket.

'That's enough for now. It's time for sleep.' Papa sat back in the chair and flicked a finger at Malik, indicating that he should lie down on the mattress. 'I hope you're not hungry. We only have a little food and we should save it.'

Malik put his head on the mattress. 'I'm not hungry.'

He would have liked to eat. If he were at home he would have had a good supper, perhaps dumplings with fried potatoes. Mama would have made him hot chocolate when he went to bed. She might have given him his favourite biscuits, the ones that had jam in the middle.

The thought left Malik sad and hungrier than he really was. He tried to think of something else, remembering his bedroom at home. He had a shelf full of books and posters of his favourite films on his wall. He also had model aeroplanes, which hung by strings from the ceiling – they were perfect replicas of planes from the last war and he had painted them himself and slid the transfers from the sheet when they were still wet.

Malik closed his eyes.

The mattress smelled damp and the room was dusty.

At home his bed had clean sheets. But he was lucky to have a mattress at all. His eyes flicked open. Papa was in the chair over by the window.

Malik used his mouth to breathe. He couldn't smell the damp if he didn't use his nose . . .

Papa sat very still in the chair and watched the boy till he fell asleep.

He was tired himself. He had forgotten the effort it took to look after a child. He hadn't had to do it since Maria was a girl and even then, if he was honest, it was his wife who had brought their daughter up.

He stretched and stifled a yawn. He needed some sleep – he couldn't take another night keeping watch while Malik slept and, anyway, they were almost safe. They hadn't seen a soldier since they left the cellar that morning and it made sense that the warlords and gangsters were moving east, up into the back of the town and away from the coast.

Perhaps now that the ship was at the dock, the peacekeepers would arrive and secure the port. They might already be here. Papa thought they should be safe here in this house, but he still ought to be careful; there were no guarantees. It only took one rogue jeep, one rebel on the make, sniffing round to see what he might find. They would shoot you as soon as look at you. It didn't matter that you had a child, not if they didn't like the look of you.

He watched the sleeping boy. Malik's arms and legs were relaxed, spread out across the mattress like a spider. There was a corner that was free, down by his feet. He might be able to lay his own head there. He thought about it and dismissed the idea. He should try to stay awake, and if he slept at all then he should sleep across the door. Yes, that might do. He could use the rucksack as a pillow. If he emptied the pockets it would be soft enough for his head. He stood up and stretched out his arms. He was so tired he could sleep anywhere. It wouldn't make a difference.

He stepped softly round the mattress, holding the rucksack in one hand, taking care not to wake Malik. Then he sat down on the floor with his back to the door and took a coin from his pocket. He walked it over the back of his fingers, from one side of his hand to the other and back again. He had learned his tricks as a child, in a summer out of school when there was nothing to do but idle away the days, and once your fingers had the knack they never lost it.

But he should go easy on the boy. It was difficult to learn new tricks – it took practice. He should be pleased that Malik even wanted to try. Papa smiled at the thought of his grandson with his hand in his underpants, but then he just as quickly became sad because the truth of it was that he hardly knew the boy. These last few days had taught him that. So many of the things Malik said or did came as a complete surprise.

Papa knew he hadn't given Maria the support she might have expected, bringing her son up on her own like that. He regretted it now that he was afraid for her. And if he had spent more time with Malik when he was growing up, then he might have known what to do when he had pulled the child from the wardrobe, the boy's eyes wide with fear and the first question on his lips, 'Where's Mama?'

Papa pulled at his beard. So many questions and not enough answers. He had tried to keep the boy calm. He had given him answers when he could think of them and some of them were true.

Mama had to leave with the soldiers because they had urgent business that only she could attend to.

Mama had asked Papa to come and collect Malik from the house.

She had hidden him in the wardrobe to keep him safe till Papa got there and she would meet them at the docks in time to board the ship.

Papa had made a game of packing. That had been a good idea. He had got Malik to go around the house and find things for him. The string. The tools. The gaffer tape. They might all come in useful and it helped to keep his mind busy – Malik was calmer when he had something to do.

Papa had shown him the coin trick to pass the time. It didn't do any harm to make him believe something can disappear and reappear, as though by magic. And the boy certainly had a good imagination; Papa had noticed that. If he was given the space and time to think, who knows what questions he might ask?

Malik was determined too. Like the way he hadn't wanted to give up on the dying dog. That dog had really got to him. And that was strange. Of all the things.

Papa put the coin back in his pocket. He moved the rucksack closer to his side so he could lean against it and go to sleep. Then he remembered that the back door was still unlocked and he sighed quietly, left the bag where it was, took hold of the torch and started down the stairs.

He ran the tap in the kitchen and scooped the running water up to his lips with the palm of his hand. The droplets fell onto the empty cans below and they sounded like rain on a tin roof. Papa turned off the tap, picked up the yellow bucket, emptied the cans into the corner of the kitchen and replaced the bucket under the tap. He caught a glimpse of the stars from the window and he turned off the torch and stood at the glass to admire them. There was the North Star, Polaris. Papa looked for the Plough.

When the gate to the yard opened, Papa quickly stepped back from the window.

He saw the figure of a man enter and then a second, the outline of their felt hats sharpened by the moonlight that cast their shadows on the pale brickwork of the back wall.

Papa hurried back into the hall, felt for the bannister, climbed two stairs at a stride, and when he reached the top remembered the kitchen door to the garden was still unlocked. He hesitated in the darkness, one hand on the railing, as he heard the door creak open.

He woke Malik by holding a finger to his lips so he would know not to speak. He could see the fear in Malik's eyes as he picked him up from the mattress, but the boy didn't make a sound and Papa carried him over to the wardrobe, put him down in the corner and closed the door tight.

Malik drew his knees up under his chin. He hadn't had time to think, didn't know what was happening and he could see nothing in the pitch-dark of the wardrobe.

He listened for any sound that might give him a clue. His head became one giant ear that was primed for the faintest noise. He leaned close to the wardrobe door but heard nothing except his own heartbeat, so heavy in his chest that it felt like a hammer on an anvil. He waited, closed his eyes and concentrated.

What had happened? What could be so dangerous that Papa had hidden him in a wardrobe? Someone must have come to the house. Perhaps it was soldiers, like the last time. Malik concentrated but still heard nothing. It might not be soldiers. Soldiers would make more noise, wouldn't they?

He put a hand on the edge of the wardrobe door and pushed it open so that a crack appeared in the dark. He put his eye up close. The candlelight flickered across the floorboards and he saw Papa standing behind the open bedroom door, his knife held up close to his face in trembling fingers.

Papa was waiting to surprise them, to pounce out and attack whoever came into the bedroom. Papa would protect him.

Malik heard footsteps in the room below. One voice spoke and he heard a second voice answer. So there were at least two of them. He saw Papa fidget and the sight of him stepping from one foot to the other made Malik think of the toilet. His bladder swelled immediately to the size of a watermelon and he wished he'd gone when Papa had told him to. He put his hand to the front of his trousers and held himself and his heart beat on the top of his ribcage as though it was hoping to be let out.

He saw the edge of Papa's blade glint in the candlelight and Malik remembered how sharp it was. He'd be safe with Papa. But Papa glanced across to the wardrobe and then lowered the knife to his side. What was he doing? Papa stepped delicately from behind the door and tiptoed over to the candle. Had he changed his mind?

In the room below, the men were walking up and down, talking to one another. Why weren't they whispering? If it were Papa and Malik, they would be quieter. Much quieter.

Malik's legs were trembling. He really did need the toilet now. He was tingly and short of breath. He was ready to burst.

He watched Papa kneel and pinch the wick between his fingers. The room went dark enough that Malik could see nothing. A moment later there was a footstep, so close that Malik could have reached out and touched the foot that made it, and then the door of the wardrobe opened fully and Papa stepped quietly in beside him, pulled the door closed and slid down the wooden panel till he was crouching in the bottom of the wardrobe, his kneecaps jutting up against Malik's own, the stiff leather of his shoe pressing uncomfortably against the top of Malik's thigh.

Papa was hiding. The same as Malik. He was hiding and hoping the men would go away.

Malik clenched every muscle in his body but it was no good, he really did need the toilet and he no longer had a choice, he needed to go right now. He began to cry and his nose began to run and the tears were warm on his cheek and his trousers were warm, right there where his hand was, and everything was running water. He could already smell the urine.

He felt a moment of joy at the relief, but it was only a moment and then the shame gripped his heart so tightly it was painful and it didn't seem to matter about the men any more.

Papa touched Malik's arm, found his hand and held it tightly.

There were footsteps coming up the stairs and voices that became clearer as they came nearer. Someone entered the room and stopped just inside the bedroom door.

'There's no one here, Angelo.' It was a man's voice. 'We were wrong.'

Another set of footsteps on the stairs.

'See that? We even have a mattress to fight over.'

The men spoke casually. They weren't frightened to raise their voices. But they didn't sound like soldiers.

'First piece of luck we've had all day.'

Malik held his breath, clenched his lips together to stop the sobbing.

'What's with the rucksack?'

'Where?'

There was a pause.

'Someone must have been here.' There were a couple of quick steps on the floorboards. 'Yes. Look. There's a candle.'

Papa put his face close. Malik felt his breath on the tip of his nose when Papa wet his lips and muttered, 'I know him.' At least that's what Malik thought he said, though he couldn't be sure whether he had heard it or imagined it.

Someone said, 'You don't think . . .'

There was silence.

A floorboard creaked right beside them, then quite suddenly the door of the wardrobe flew open and a torch lit up Papa's face. His eyes blinked in the brightness, but instead of leaping out with his knife

Papa stayed where he was, crouched and flinching in the bottom of the wardrobe.

And then someone said a name. 'Salvatore? Is that you? Salvatore Bartholomew?'

Papa took a deep breath and opened his eyes. 'Hector Valentine!' Papa struggled to stand up. He stepped from the wardrobe and the torchlight followed his face. Malik crouched in the dark corner of the wardrobe, watching the men, unsure whether they had seen him or not.

Papa brushed his clothes with the back of his hand in an attempt to salvage some dignity. He spoke as though they were all meeting up in a bar or a café. 'What are you doing scaring an elderly man in the middle of the night?'

Hector Valentine hugged him. 'I don't believe it!' He laughed loudly and let Papa go. 'Salvatore! You're alive. No, I really can't believe it. Alive and well. And sitting in a wardrobe at the docks. Ha! Who would believe it? Are you here for the ship?'

Papa let go of the man. 'Yes. Of course. And you too?'

Hector took off his hat. He was a lot younger than Papa. He had a side parting that threw a large wedge of brown hair onto the forehead above his tortoiseshell spectacles – it bobbed as he shook his head. 'Yes. Yes, of course. We're here for the ship as well.' He gestured to the man who held the torch on them both. 'Salvatore, this is Angelo Vex. Perhaps you already know one another?'

Malik could only see the shadow of a man, a silhouette of his hat and jawbone.

Papa gave a little bow. 'I know the name.'

Hector turned from one man to the other. 'Vex, this is a friend of mine, Salvatore Bartholomew. An old client of many years. He runs a factory over on the east side, up near the Terminus.'

Papa beamed. 'I employ over thirty people. It's manufacturing mostly. Import, export.'

Angelo Vex smiled. 'That's impressive.' He held a hand out. 'It's good to meet you.'

Papa shook his hand, but then Vex swung the torch over into the wardrobe. 'Is someone else in there?'

Malik closed his eyes from the light. He didn't want to come out. He wanted the men to go away. He shifted in the bottom of the damp wardrobe.

'Malik!' Papa reached inside and took hold of Malik's arm. 'I'm sorry. I had quite forgotten you. Stand up, Malik. Stand up and meet our friends.'

Hector turned to the wardrobe. 'Is Malik here as well?' He took hold of Malik's other arm and helped him step out onto the floor. 'Come out, Malik. Come out and let me see you.' Hector slapped his back. 'It's been a long time. Two years at least.'

Malik wouldn't look at the men. He stared at his bare feet.

'I believe he may have wet himself,' said Angelo Vex matter-of-factly.

'Oh dear. Yes, I am so sorry,' Papa apologized. He fumbled for a handkerchief in his pocket and handed it to Malik. 'We were both very scared. We thought you might be . . . well . . . you can imagine, I am sure . . . Come on, Malik. Come with me. There's water in the kitchen.' He took hold of Malik's arm again. 'Do you have your torch?'

'Here, take this one.' Vex offered them his torch.

'Thank you, thank you. But here, I have a lighter. Let me light the candle for you. I can't leave the two of you in darkness. The curtain blocks out the light, so it's quite safe.'

Papa relit the wick, picked up the rucksack and led Malik downstairs to the kitchen. Malik stood just inside the door, waiting for Papa to fill the bucket with water before he removed his pants, and then he held the wet clothes at arm's length, the tails of his white shirt covering the tops of his thin, naked legs.

'Wash yourself down while I find your clean clothes,' said Papa.

Malik did what he was told, then put on the dry clothes while Papa washed the wet trousers, scrubbing the legs together roughly.

'This isn't perfect but it will have to do.' Papa pushed the trousers back under the surface and rubbed again. 'Soap. That's something else I forgot to put in the rucksack.'

Mama used lavender soap at home. Malik wished she was here washing his clothes.

'Do you mind wearing short trousers?'

'I don't mind.' Malik preferred short trousers. 'Why are the men here?' It felt different now they were with them. He didn't like it. He wanted them to leave.

'They're hiding, Malik. Just like us. Hiding until the time is right to board the ship. You must recognize one of them? No? Not Hector Valentine? He's been to the house for parties. He's the family lawyer, worked for me since I set up in business.'

Malik remembered the parties at Papa's house.

He held them twice a year, once at Christmas and once in the summer, and Malik had been expected to attend with his mother, though he never liked to go. There were always too many people and none of them were children, but Papa liked to show Malik off to his guests and he would have to stand at Papa's side, breathing in smoke from their cigars.

No, he couldn't remember Hector and he didn't see why he should.

Papa wrung out Malik's trousers and hung them on a metal bracket that jutted from the wall. He dangled the underpants from the handle of the back door. 'I have never met Angelo Vex, but I know his reputation. He's a very important man, Malik. Very wealthy. They say he started out selling fruit and vegetables from a market stall. He must have been some trader, eh? To go from selling fruit to where he is now.'

Malik didn't care.

'This is a stroke of luck. Believe me, Malik, a real stroke of luck.'

Papa reached across, took hold of Malik's shoulder and turned him round to face the stairs. 'Let's go and see what they have to say for themselves.'

The two men had removed their hats. They were sitting on the floor with the candle between them.

'Come in,' said Hector.

Angelo Vex motioned to Papa. 'We thought the chair must be yours. Come and sit down. And the bed is for you?' He beckoned Malik to the mattress and Malik went and squatted on the edge. He took his first proper look at Vex and saw a man in his forties with an athletic build and hair that was thinning at the crown of his head.

It felt like these men had made the room their own and now Malik was their guest. Papa pulled his chair closer to the pair of them. Hector had set the full ashtray in front of him, together with an open carton of cigarettes and a silver lighter. He took one out and lit it. Malik watched the smoke curl over toward him.

Hector turned to Papa. 'You must tell us everything, Salvatore. How did you get here? How long have you been here?'

Papa leaned forward. 'We only arrived at the house a few hours ago. It has taken us two days walking.'

'Two days? From where?'

'From the suburbs in the west. We found our way through the back streets but it wasn't easy.'

Vex scratched at his short moustache and Malik saw he had a fingernail that was black and pointed and longer than the rest. 'Did you notice the Stock Exchange? I heard it was burning.'

Papa nodded. 'We had to go out of our way because of it. And it's not alone. There isn't a bank that isn't burning. Not a shop or a business that hasn't been ransacked.'

Vex shook his head. 'They're going through the place like rats. They blame the bankers and the businessmen, but what can *we* do? I tell you, I'm glad I got my family away when I did. All of my accounts are frozen. I found out three days ago. The money has all gone. Vanished.'

Hector blew smoke across the room. 'That's not legal, either. I should know. But they can do as they please. I have also lost everything.'

Papa nodded as though he knew it was the same for everyone. 'And how is it you're together?'

'We met at the docks just this afternoon.'

'Ah,' said Papa.

Malik felt a dull ache in his stomach. Perhaps he was hungry.

Hector tapped some ash from the tip of his cigarette. 'And what about Maria? Is it just the two of you?'

Malik sat up straight at the mention of his mother's name and Papa glanced across at him. 'She's not with us. She had some things to see to, but she will meet us at the ship tomorrow.'

Hector looked concerned. 'But we've been told that the ship won't leave tomorrow.'

'What do you mean?'

'They have changed its schedule.' Hector stubbed the end of his cigarette into the ashtray. 'The ship won't leave now till the following morning. The peacekeepers must secure the port and supervise the evacuation, but that will give time for more people to arrive and that may make things difficult for those of us without tickets.'

Malik could tell that Papa knew nothing of this. His grandfather had nothing but questions: 'How can you know such a thing? Who told you this?' Papa had raised his voice. He glanced over at the window before whispering, 'There have been many different rumours.'

'We've been to the docks,' said Hector. 'We've spoken to the official who will allocate places on the ship.'

'And who is that? I use the port a lot for my work. Perhaps I know him.'

The two men hesitated. 'It is Nicholas Massa who has the last word.'

Papa threw his hand up in disgust. 'The man from the council?' He shook his head. 'He's a crook! Always has been. He's more guilty than anyone for this mess. How can he be involved?'

Hector shrugged. 'He must intend to stay and fight it out. He has a finger in every pie – he always has had. Good luck to him, I say –'

'I know this man,' interrupted Vex. 'I once did him a favour.'

'And will that help you?' asked Papa quickly. Malik didn't like Papa asking so many questions.

Vex shrugged his shoulders. 'Perhaps it will count for something, but unless we have money it won't count for much.'

Papa looked quickly from one man to the other and back again. 'No one said anything about money. They said this was a ship that had come to take families and children. They said it would take orphans.'

'Yes, yes,' said Hector. 'A charity has sponsored some places for orphans. But most of the other places will be sold for cash. It's always the way. Nothing is ever assured in life unless you can pay for it.'

'And do you have the money? Have the two of you already bought tickets?' Papa was agitated and didn't wait for the answer. 'I mean, I have some money – it's not much, but I had thought it might be enough for me and the boy if we needed it.'

'How much do you have?' asked Hector. 'If you don't mind me asking?'

Papa stood up. He took a leather wallet from his trouser pocket and opened it, took a fistful of notes from the back, sat down on the chair and leaned forward into the huddle of men. He held the money up. 'Surely this is enough?' Malik saw the two men exchange looks and Papa saw it too. 'For heaven's sake, I'm not trying to buy the ship.' Papa laughed at his own joke, then stopped abruptly. 'Listen, I don't doubt what you say. It makes sense. It's always about contacts.' He lowered his voice and bent closer to the centre of their circle. 'But how much? Did Massa tell you the price of a ticket?'

Malik leaned forward in case Hector whispered.

'Ten thousand.' Hector said it clearly. 'That was the price.'

Papa dropped the money he was holding into his lap. 'Good God, I hadn't expected that.'

Hector stood up and walked over to the window. 'What did you expect?'

'I don't know.' Papa tugged at his beard. 'But I didn't expect that.'

'How much have you got there?' asked Vex. 'Perhaps we should all count our cash?'

Hector took a wallet from his pocket and Vex opened up a leather satchel that he had left on the floor and took out a silver clip of notes. The men moved closer together in the candlelight, slipping banknotes from one hand to the other, muttering figures under their breath.

Hector declared his hand first. 'Two thousand, four hundred and fifty.'

Vex said, 'Exactly eighteen hundred.'

Papa shook his head, 'I have four thousand, one hundred.' He looked apologetic. 'It's not enough.'

Malik remembered the money he had back at home. He had kept it in a box in the chest of drawers in his bedroom, but he knew it was less than a hundred and he'd spent some of that on a book about steam trains. It wouldn't be enough, either. 'Mama might have some money when she arrives,' he added helpfully.

The men didn't respond.

Vex traced the gap between the floorboards with his finger and Hector had pulled the curtain back from the window and was watching the street.

Papa had sat back in the chair and was tugging at his short white beard. Then, out of nothing, he said, 'Would it be cheaper for four people?'

'For five, Papa.' Malik was suddenly alert. 'There will be five of us with Mama.'

'Yes. You're right. See what's happened to me?' Papa gave a short laugh. He watched Vex intently. 'Would there be a discount if there were five of us?'

Vex appeared to have lost interest in the whole thing. He answered Papa with a sweep of his hand. 'There's no discount. Massa could sell the tickets five times over, I am sure. He would be doing me a favour simply by selling them to us, but we haven't the money.'

Papa nodded. 'Of course,' he said. 'Yes, yes. Of course.' He put his head in his hands and looked at the floor and the room returned to silence.

Even Malik couldn't think of a question.

He wanted to be alone. No, not alone, that would be too frightening, but he wanted to be on his own with Papa. He wanted the men to leave.

He wondered where they would sleep if they

stayed. Surely Papa wouldn't let them stay here in this room? He would send them downstairs at the very least? But Papa showed no inclination to either speak or move. He was sitting in the chair and he was thinking. He hung his head and held onto his beard and Malik felt forgotten by him.

And he was still hungry.

Malik's stomach began to make a sound like the radiators did at school when they had only just come on. He wondered if Papa had heard it. Perhaps it was a good time to ask for one of the apples in his pocket.

In the centre of the floor, the candle flickered and its light jigged across the floorboards. Suddenly Papa stood up. He looked at Vex, wagged a finger and smiled. 'I know who you are.' He walked closer to him. 'I have heard your name spoken in all the right circles. I didn't like to say anything and it's none of my business, but people say you are very rich.' Even in the candlelight, Malik could see that Papa had a glint in his eye. He smiled craftily. 'You must be very well connected to go from a market stall to where you are now.'

Vex shook his head, annoyed. He pointed a finger back at Papa. 'No, I really must . . . I have to contradict you. That is a story which persists in following me however much I refute it.' He came close to Papa and fixed his eyes on his face. 'I have never owned a market stall. Please believe me. I made my money from an idea, a very simple idea – although, yes, I grant you, it did concern a vegetable.' Vex stood toe to toe with Papa. He cupped his hand and held it up between them as though he were holding a cricket ball. 'I noticed that an onion appeared to have a far greater volume when chopped than it does when it is whole. I bought my onions cheaply, chopped them, then packaged them as instant ingredients: healthier than fast food, but convenient. It's a modern idea.' He glanced at Malik as though he should be young enough to understand. 'I marketed them to appeal to those people who believed they didn't have the energy or the time to chop an onion.' He raised an eyebrow. 'Do you see? I sold them the *idea* of an onion rather than the onion itself. I sold a lifestyle. I made a simple foodstuff into a luxury product and sold my onion for forty times what it cost me.' He smiled with satisfaction. 'Of course, I have moved into very different fields since then – banking, selling bonds, that kind of thing – but I believe that is probably where this myth of the market stall comes from.'

Malik could see that Papa was flustered at being given such a speech. 'Yes, I understand,' Papa said. 'Luxury vegetables. That's clever. I see that. But my point was that with everything you have built, with all that you have become, well, that can't simply disappear. Surely not?'

Papa paused with his hands held out, waiting like a dog for a bone, but Vex gave him nothing.

Papa became impatient. He took hold of Vex's shoulder. 'You are a great man. You must still have influence. You *must* have items of value.' Papa's eyes searched his face for a sign that it was true. 'For God's sake, is there nothing you could sell? What about your houses? There must be something you can do?' He lowered his voice. 'I will be good for credit when we are safely away – I can assure you of that.'

Vex took the old man's hand and squeezed it. 'You're very kind but you flatter me.' He stepped away from Papa, and Malik caught a glimpse of shoes that were polished. 'Not so long ago that would have been true. Only a month ago I could have sailed away in the best cabin on the ship.' Vex shook his head. 'But not now. Would I be here if that were still the case? No, I wouldn't. I expect I would already be on the ship. Instead, I have been at the docks and I have stood in a line on the quayside with everybody else, waiting to see the likes of Nicholas Massa, hoping I can find someone that I know who will help.' He sucked at the gap in his front teeth. 'I saw Martin Krupp in the same queue.'

'The town clerk?'

'The same. One of the most connected men in the town.'

'He was a rich man,' added Hector, as though he were reminiscing of a warm summer's day.

'I saw Kolarov too, the owner of DBG. I saw Cohen from Adams and Cork. You should have seen them – you would not have believed it. Their faces were dirty, their clothes torn. They looked like dockers, but then I suppose I do too.' He opened his arms, inviting them to look at his clothing. 'Do you see how I am dressed these days?'

Vex turned a full circle, and even in the candle-light they could tell that his clothes were old and un-ironed. Malik noticed a hole in the knee of Vex's trousers, but he looked again at the expensive shoes.

Vex put his hands in his jacket pockets. 'We were all rich men once. No? We have all seen the good times. But not any more.'

Malik didn't like listening to this. It only made him more anxious. He was really hungry now. If only these men would leave then he could ask Papa for some food. When it was just him and Papa, it had been simple. And if Mama were here then she would make everything all right because she always did. Malik wished he'd never hidden when she had told him to. He should have stayed close to her. He should have held her hand and never let her go.

'Papa, I'm hungry,' he said.

Papa appeared to have forgotten that Malik was even there. 'You must wait for the morning,' he said. 'You should be sleeping now. Come on. Lie down and try to get some sleep.'

Hector produced a cereal bar from his jacket pocket and walked over to the mattress. 'Here.' He handed it to Malik. 'I've already eaten today, so it's better that you have it. I can buy food tomorrow. I saw a woman on the docks selling melons from a bucket and I have enough money.' He laughed. 'So, that's the good news for today, gentlemen.' He held his arms out wide. 'Even in times like these, I can still afford a melon for my supper.'

Malik held the bar by the edge of the wrapper but

he didn't open it. Now he felt bad about wishing the men weren't here.

Papa looked over. 'Thank Hector for the food, Malik.'

Malik tore the end off the foil. 'Thank you.' He took a bite. The bar tasted of nuts and honey and oatmeal.

Vex went over to his satchel. 'If you're hungry you should have these as well.' He produced an orange and a brown paper bag, twisted at each corner to keep it sealed. He looked embarrassed. 'I've also eaten today.'

Papa took the food, untwisted the paper bag and looked inside. 'A sandwich. Thank you. You are good men. Good men.' His face sparkled when he smiled. 'Thank you.' He handed one half of the sandwich to Malik, who lifted the bread and saw cheese and ham inside. Papa offered to return the other half. 'You should take this back. I think you're too generous. Far too generous.'

'Not at all,' said Vex. 'You haven't eaten. Go on. Take the other half for yourself. But perhaps we could all share the orange? I find it refreshes the mouth if I've been smoking.'

Papa handed the orange back to Vex, who dug his

long nail into the pitted skin and peeled it in a single piece which he placed by the ashtray. He parted the flesh into sections, then bowed his head and blessed the food. Papa turned the sandwich in his fingers to hide the bite he had already taken.

Malik could smell the juice on his fingers as he held his piece of the orange, and he popped it in his mouth and chewed. The food tasted good and the tang of cheese and orange stayed on his teeth long after he had finished and he sucked at them, reminded of lunches in cafés and afternoon outings to the beach with Mama.

'I should go.' Vex took them by surprise. He crouched down to the candle and picked up his bag.

Papa was startled. 'Please . . . no, wait . . . don't go yet.' He knelt next to Vex and put a hand around his. 'There's something else. Something you should know.'

Vex raised his eyebrows and waited. Malik sat up straighter and tucked his legs under him on the mattress.

Now that everyone was looking at him, Papa seemed to want to take back his words. He hesitated, looked at each of their faces in turn then said, 'There may be a way for us to get the tickets. It's only a chance . . . but . . .'

'Salvatore?' asked Hector. He walked back from the window and stood over the two crouching men. 'Salvatore, what do you have in mind?'

Malik knew that Papa would find a way. He knew it.

Papa still had his fingers over Vex's hand. He suddenly seemed to notice and let go. 'I have something you should see, something of great value.'

He stood up and walked to the corner of the room and then he came back to the candle. 'It may be worth enough to get tickets for us all. Yes, I'm sure it is. I should have said something, I know that now, but well, it's something of a last resort, a little nest egg which I hadn't intended to use. I hope you will understand why I didn't say anything earlier.'

Everyone waited expectantly.

'What is it?' Hector was anxious. 'You have to tell us.'

Malik had moved to the edge of the mattress and Papa waved him closer to the chair. 'Malik? Do you have the torch with you? Bring it here to me.'

Malik brought the torch across to Papa but Papa didn't take it from him. Instead, he stretched out his legs to make himself comfortable and put his hands on his thighs. He had a smile on his face. 'You haven't guessed yet, eh?' Papa's eyes sparkled and Malik felt like it should be Christmas or his birthday, but that was confusing. He didn't want Papa to play games with him like this.

'What is it, Papa?'

Papa ruffled Malik's hair. 'All this time with your old Papa and you never knew. Well, you're in for a shock, my boy. It's some sight, I can tell you.' Malik edged closer to him. 'Turn on the torch. Go on. There. That's it. Now . . .' He put a finger to his face and pointed to his mouth. 'Shine it here. Right in the back of my mouth.'

Papa tipped his head back and Malik tilted forward with the torch. He saw Papa's eyes swivel in their sockets to follow him as he came in close.

'Look properly,' said Papa. Hector and Vex edged around behind Malik's shoulders, trying to see what was there. 'Can you see it?'

Papa opened his mouth wider and Malik held the torch next to Papa's lips, and when he bent in close he saw it straightaway, a sudden flash of brilliance at the back of the teeth. Malik gasped and pulled away.

'What is it?' Hector leaned over Malik's shoulder. 'Let me look.' He brushed Malik aside and took hold of the torch. He put his head close to Papa's mouth and peered inside. 'A diamond! Vex, come and see. It really is.' Hector laughed out loud. 'It's a diamond!'

Vex nudged Hector out of the way and grasped the torch. He placed a hand on Papa's forehead to keep his head pushed back. 'Good God. It really is. That's some jewel. How big is that?'

Vex released Papa's head so he could talk. 'It's the biggest I could find that would fit comfortably in my mouth. I had it set into the tooth.'

Hector took the torch from Vex. 'Let me see it again.' He made Papa open his mouth by tugging at his beard and Malik caught a second glimpse of the diamond nestling at the back of Papa's mouth, a ribbon of saliva around the gums.

'I don't believe it!' Hector's own mouth hung open. 'Just look at the size of it.' He shook his head in disbelief and began to laugh. Then he let go of Papa's chin and wheeled away across the room. 'When did you put it in there?'

Vex stepped up to have another look but Papa closed his mouth. 'Enough.' He waved both men away. 'Could I have some water please, Malik?'

Malik brought back the flask from the rucksack and Papa unscrewed the cap and took a decent swig. He gasped when he was finished. 'I had the jewel set in my tooth three months ago when the banks began to default on loans. I saw what was about to happen, knew it would turn out like this, and so I sold my house.' He reached across and touched Vex's sleeve. 'I took a hefty blow on its true value, but I knew that it would soon be worth nothing to me and so I made sure of a quick sale and got paid in cash. I also withdrew my savings from the bank.'

'Did you sell the business?' asked Hector.

Papa shook his head. 'There was no time.'

'How did you find such a jewel?'

'I had to go to the diamond traders out east and I had my dentist set it into the tooth, where nobody would think to look. I had planned it as a new start. It was my insurance – a little something set aside for once we got away from here.' Papa raised his eyebrows. 'I wouldn't want to rely on the generosity of others. You know how it is.'

'You're a sly old dog,' said Hector.

'And this way there's no export tax to pay on it.' Vex ran his tongue across his lower lip.

Papa chuckled. 'Yes, it was a clever thing to do.

I'm sure of that.' He looked across to see if Malik was taking it all in and Malik smiled back at him. Mama would be smiling too once she knew.

'But now I see I need a change of plan.' Papa slapped his hands against the top of his thighs. 'If we can't get on the ship then it's nothing more than an expensive filling.' He leaned down and put the flask of water on the floor, and when he straightened up he held his arms out in a grand gesture, intended to hold them all. 'And so tomorrow, gentlemen, I shall go to see the very same dentist, I shall pay him to remove the diamond and then I shall sell it.' Papa winked at Malik. 'We will have more than enough money for the tickets and I intend to buy five.' He stood up from the chair and hugged each of them in turn. 'That will be one for each of us. Perhaps I shall ask for cabins. Why not? We could travel first-class. And I mean to get a discount.'

'That's very generous of you, Salvatore.' Hector bent down and ruffled Malik's hair. 'See what a clever man your papa is?'

Malik couldn't keep the smile from his face. He had known that Papa would know what to do.

Papa laughed. He patted his stomach as though he had just eaten a good meal rather than half a sandwich and a segment of orange. 'Money will buy you a good-looking dog, Hector, but generosity will get him to wag his tail. That's worth remembering.'

Vex had walked away and was standing quietly at the door. He had his back to them when he pointed a finger in the air and said loudly, 'No.' He turned back to the room and shook his head at them. 'It won't work.'

Papa was incredulous. 'Of course it will work. It's worth one hundred thousand at the very least – enough to buy tickets for all of us. I'm sure of that.'

'I don't doubt it.' Vex had a hand to his chin, the way Papa did when he was thinking. 'I have bought and sold diamonds and I know their value.' He walked back across the room and stood over Papa. 'But what are the chances of finding a dentist tomorrow? The whole world has gone mad. Your dentist will live . . . where? I don't know, let's say . . .'

'The old town.' Papa leaned forward in his chair. 'He lives and works in the old town. Most of them do. If we can't find him, there will be another.'

'But there is no old town. Not any more. You more or less said so yourself.' Vex ran his hand across the hair that was left on his head. 'What are the chances of us finding someone who will do it? We have more chance of finding a dentist at the dock, waiting to board the ship.'

'That's not a bad idea,' cried Hector. He flicked back the hair from the front of his face. 'We can go first thing in the morning and ask around till we find someone.'

Vex shook his head. 'Even if we find someone they will have no anaesthetic, no drills and nowhere to perform the operation. And he has to be trust-worthy. It can't be just anyone.'

They paused, the one man looking to the other.

'Mama always takes me to the dentist,' Malik suggested, trying to be helpful. 'She might know where you can go, Papa.'

The men ignored him. All three of them stared at the floor and Malik watched them with a growing sense of unease. Eventually Papa shook his head. 'Vex is right.' He spoke more to himself than to anyone in particular. 'What was I thinking of?'

'We should at least try.' Hector walked round to the mattress. He reached down and put a hand on Malik's shoulder to reassure him. 'It's the only thing we can do.'

'It'll take too long.' Papa shook his head. 'We may not have the time needed to sell the jewel and still get tickets for the ship. That's something else we should consider.'

Vex crouched in front of Papa. He put a hand on his knee. 'Let me look again.' He had assumed the authority of a professional and Papa opened his mouth without question. Vex stared at the jewel. 'Do you mind me doing this?' He put a finger past Papa's front teeth and prodded, then wiped his finger on the leg of his trousers. He stood up. 'There is another way,' he declared.

'What do you mean?' asked Hector.

Vex put his hands up as though he were surrendering. 'It's not for me to say.'

Papa stared up at him calmly. 'I'd rather you said it.'

Vex nodded slowly. 'I think you know what I have in mind.'

'Say it anyway. It's easier for you to say it.'

Malik had no idea what they were talking about.

Vex shrugged. 'I think it's possible for us to take the tooth out ourselves.'

Papa smiled ruefully. 'It's the obvious thing to do.'

Vex was reassured that Papa agreed. He came quickly across and slapped him on the shoulder, smiling as though it had all been decided. 'If we're lucky, old man, it won't be too hard.'

Hector looked at Vex. 'You're not serious? How will you do it?'

'Hey. Not so fast, eh!' Papa looked worried and he wouldn't meet their eyes. 'I have always had strong teeth. It might not be so easy. Let me think of a better way.' Papa leaned forward in the chair, put his elbow on his knee and sat with his fingers across his mouth.

Malik held his breath.

Papa said, 'Couldn't we find a wealthy passenger to buy our tickets and accompany us onto the ship?' Papa looked eagerly between the two men. 'I could go straight to the dentist once we arrived, then I could pay them back in cash. Whoever did it would make a lot of money.'

Vex shook his head. 'There's too much risk. I wouldn't do it. Not in these circumstances. If I could hold the diamond in my hand and say it's mine, then that would be a different matter.'

Malik saw the resignation spread across Papa's face. He went and took hold of Papa's hand and squeezed his fingers, just like Mama might have done for him if she were here.

Papa smiled weakly then he took his hand from Malik's. 'I know you're right.' He nodded at Vex. 'So we must do it ourselves.' He flicked a finger at Hector. 'Bring me my rucksack, will you?'

Hector brought him the bag and they watched Papa unzip the large side pocket where he had stored his tools. He laid out the hammer, the pliers and the screwdriver on the wooden floorboards behind the candle. 'Show me your hands.'

The three of them put out their hands. Malik could see that Vex's fingers were rough, with a patch of dead skin up near the long black nail. Hector's hands were gentler, although he had a callus on the edge of the finger where he must have held his pen. Papa looked at each of them and then turned to Hector. 'You've never done a hard day's work in your life, Hector, but your hands are smaller than Angelo's . . . perhaps you will be more precise.'

'Good God. Are you sure?' Hector took a deep breath.

He bent down and chose the pliers. 'I think these will be best, don't you?'

He felt the weight of them, pulled the jaws open, then snapped them shut – Malik was reminded of the crocodile in *Peter Pan*. He sat down beside Papa and held his fingers.

Hector took a deep breath and looked at Vex. 'I'll need you to hold the torch.'

Vex nodded and touched Malik's head with a finger. 'You should come away.'

Malik sat back on the edge of the mattress. He didn't want them to do it and he tried to think of something to say that would change their minds. But if this meant they could get on the ship, well, maybe it was worth it. He had to trust Papa.

The two men stood over Papa's chair and the candlelight threw their shadows up against the wall. Malik brought his knees right up into his chest and held them in his arms. 'Will it hurt?' he asked.

'Yes,' said Vex. He walked around behind Papa. 'But not for very long. If we're quick, it'll be over and done with before we know it, so let's do it now, before we change our minds.'

The men all agreed.

Vex took hold of Papa's forehead so that he held him in a headlock, and with his other hand he held the torch in front of Papa's mouth. Hector tested the pliers one last time, then he leaned across, hooked a finger inside Papa's cheek and stretched his mouth out so he could see the tooth. Papa tensed and Vex tightened the grip on his head.

Malik didn't want to watch, but he couldn't look away as Hector guided the pliers into Papa's mouth. He squeezed the handles and Malik heard them scrape against bone and come together with a click. Papa struggled. He brought up a hand and yanked the pliers away, then his fingers scratched at Vex's arm and he choked on his own spit.

'Let him go!' Hector shouted. 'Let him go, for God's sake.'

Vex freed Papa's head and Papa spilled forward over his own knees, gagging. He spat onto the floor and gasped for breath.

Malik edged closer, unsure what had happened. 'Did you do it?'

'I didn't get the chance.' Hector sounded angry. 'Why did you bring your hand up?'

Papa had a finger inside his mouth, feeling his gums. 'I couldn't help it,' he wheezed. 'I was choking. My tongue went to the back of my throat.'

Vex was calm. He put an arm round both of their shoulders. 'You must be quicker,' he told Hector. He went and stood again at the back of Papa's chair. 'Again. We must try again.'

Malik moved to the far end of the mattress. He wouldn't look this time. He put his hands over his ears and shut his eyes tight. He counted to ten, then thought it wouldn't be long enough, so he counted again, this time out loud so he wouldn't hear the muffled grunts and gasps that had begun.

When he took his hands away and opened his eyes, the men were arguing.

Hector blamed Vex. 'You should have held his hands down.'

'How can I hold his hands and his head at the same time?'

Papa looked as though he'd just run for a bus. His face was red and he was short of breath. He ran a finger across the front of his teeth and when he brought it away there was blood. He apologized. 'I'm sorry.' He wiped his finger on his trousers. 'I have never been brave.'

Hector was exasperated. 'But you must try, Salvatore.' He looked across at Malik. 'You have to do it for the boy. Think of Malik. It's his only chance of getting on the ship. If we arrive tomorrow without money then there's no hope for him.'

'We're all relying on you,' said Vex. 'But I disagree. I think you are a very brave man indeed.'

Papa looked grateful. Having Vex say such a thing seemed to give him more resolve and he pointed to the floor. 'Bring me my sack again.' He took the ball of thick yellow twine from the same pocket that he had the tools. He handed it over his head to Vex. 'You must tie me to the chair – it's the only way. Tie me tightly and let's get this over with.'

Vex loosened the end of the twine and stepped back so he could weigh up both the man and the chair he sat in. He crouched down and took hold of Papa's ankle and Papa let his shin be put against the wooden leg. Vex wound the twine around a good many times before he tied it off.

Malik held his own wrist in his fingers as he watched Papa become increasingly helpless. 'I don't like it,' he said quietly, and he lay down on the mattress and curled his knees up into his chest.

Papa smiled weakly. 'It's not as bad as it looks.' He held his hands calmly in his lap and Vex parted them and put one on either side of the chair and he tied them round the wrist and then again round the wood, at the joint where the seat met the legs.

When Vex had finished, Papa could move nothing but his head. Vex stood back and looked over his work.

'You've used a lot of twine,' Papa tutted. 'That'll take some time to roll up when we're done, but we shouldn't waste it.' He put his head back. 'Please be quick.'

Hector approached the chair with a new look of determination, and Malik closed his eyes. He could hear Papa's breath quicken. Then Papa began to choke. 'Twist them, man!' shouted Vex. 'Pull the handles back!'

'Aaargh.' Papa began to make a strange strangled kind of noise as though someone had their hands around his throat.

Malik kept his eyes tight shut. A foot stamped hard on the floorboards.

'Stop it!' Malik shouted and he put his hands over his ears.

'Aaargh!' screamed Papa again and Hector let out a scream of his own. 'Aaargh!'

There was a loud crash and someone cursed at the top of their voice: 'Oh, for crying out loud!'

Malik took his hands from his head and opened his eyes.

Hector was on his backside, sprawled out across the floorboards. 'He bit me.' He lifted a bloody hand and shook it at Papa. 'You bit my finger like an animal.'

Malik went to Papa, who sat in the chair with his head hanging to one side. He looked weak. He was breathing heavily and the front of his white shirt had a napkin of blood. Malik put a hand to his face.

Behind them, Vex was shouting at Hector. 'You're useless.' He pulled the accountant to his feet and slapped his face. 'Get up and hold his head. I can see I'll have to do it myself.'

Malik stood in the way. 'Stop it,' he said.

'Almost there, Malik,' Papa said weakly. 'Let them be.'

Malik ran across the room and out of the door. He was halfway down the stairs before he stopped in the darkness, realizing he had nowhere to go and no one to ask for help. At the top of the stairs, the candlelight flickered in the bedroom doorway.

'Tighter,' ordered Vex. There was a scrape as the pliers were picked up from the floor.

Malik crept back up the stairs and stood at the open door. Hector had a hold of Papa's head and in his other hand he held the torch high over Papa's face. Vex had two fingers inside Papa's cheek to stretch it out wide. He put the pliers in Papa's mouth. 'Let go of the torch,' he ordered, and Hector dropped the torch to the floor and held onto Papa's head with both hands, spreading his feet wider on the floor to steady himself.

Vex tightened his grip on the pliers, moving carefully and slowly. Then suddenly he twisted.

'Aaaargh . . . !' Papa came to life and his eyes went wide. He screamed loudly, and Vex's arm shook with the effort. 'Aaaargh . . . !'

Vex put a foot up on the chair and his body arched over Papa.

'Aaaargh . . . !'

Malik stared at Papa's hands, watched them curl and clench the leg of the chair as his fingers became hard white claws.

The two men screamed together, so close now they could have been one person, with Hector behind them holding Papa's head, his eyes tight shut, his own teeth clenched.

'*Aaaaargh!*'

Then suddenly Vex separated. He pulled the pliers from Papa's mouth and stepped away so that Papa fell forward, the chair tipping with him until Hector caught hold of his collar and pulled the chair back onto four feet.

'It's over,' said Vex. He bent down and picked the torch up from the floor, then straightened himself and lifted the pliers into the beam of light. There was the diamond, glistening in the torchlight, and hanging from it was the root of Papa's tooth, like a prize taken from an animal, with the blood still smeared across it.

Malik stepped inside the room again.

Vex took hold of the diamond between his thumb and forefinger and Hector was suddenly there at his side, the two of them standing toe to toe, staring at the stone that Vex held up between them, only centimetres from their eyes.

'Untie me.' Papa's voice was weak and tired. 'Please, untie me.'

Malik ran across to the chair and took the penknife from his pocket. He opened the longest blade and began to cut at the twine round Papa's wrists, sawing as fast as he could, loosing first one hand and then the second, one ankle and then the next.

Papa was pale, his head still bowed. He shook as though he were cold, with tiny tremors that shivered across his shoulders and around his open mouth. He wasn't strong enough to lift his chin from his chest.

Malik was aware that Hector and Vex were still staring at the jewel.

'Shall we chisel the tooth away?' asked Hector.

'I can't decide.' Vex closed his fingers around the tooth. 'We might damage the stone. Better to sell it as it is. Let them do it.'

'How will they weigh it like this?'

'They won't need to weigh it.' Vex felt the weight of the stone in his palm. 'I can see the value of it. I'll know the price.'

'Let me see it.' Papa's voice was weak but determined. He lifted his chin and his eyes turned toward them. Malik cut quickly at the twine, then Papa reached out a hand and tugged at Hector's sleeve and the men turned round, surprised.

Papa's face was white but his eyes were clear. His beard glistened bright red in the candlelight. A single strand of twine still held Papa to the chair and Malik sliced through it. Papa lurched forward but then regained his balance and stretched out a hand, half rising to his feet, too weak to properly stand.

He flexed his fingers at the men. 'Let me have it.'

Vex hesitated, seeming to weigh it one last time before he put the tooth into Papa's hand.

Papa closed his fingers round the diamond. 'There,' he said, and he held it up to his eye to see it glisten. 'There,' he said again. 'Now we have done it.'

The morning sun rose quickly, dispatching the long night that hung across the bows of the ship down at the dock. The sunlight lifted the gloom from the cracks between the cobbles of the street. It brightened the colour of the doors and windows in the cottages and crept around the half-shut curtain of the upstairs room and across the wooden floor.

Malik opened his eyes when the sunlight warmed his face. Papa's head was lying close to his own. He was asleep on his back, his body slung across the bare floorboards, his mouth wide open. A line of saliva dribbled from the corner of his lips, which had swollen into patches of purple, red and blue, and he was breathing heavily.

Malik sat up and looked around the room. He was alone with Papa. He got to his feet, walked to the window and pulled the curtain back to make the room brighter. The street was empty. Above the opposite cottage he could see thin white clouds in a pale blue sky. A coil of dark smoke rose into the air from the back of the town.

Malik stepped into his Wellington boots and stood over Papa, expecting him to wake. He thought

Papa looked older when he was asleep. The bright sunlight showed blood, like tiny flakes of rust, still clinging to the hairs of Papa's white beard. Hector had helped Papa wash himself, using water that Malik had brought up in the bucket, and in the dim light of the candle they had thought his beard was clean. Papa's shirt still lay in the corner of the room where Hector had thrown it, saying, 'You'll never get the blood out of that, but don't worry – now you have the money to buy as many shirts as you want.'

Malik decided to let Papa sleep.

He went downstairs, expecting to see Hector and Vex. He thought they would be in the sitting room but found it was empty. They weren't in the kitchen either. When he turned the handle on the back door, he found it unlocked. That was strange. He put his head outside. In daylight, the yard was smaller than he had imagined and empty, with the exception of a wooden planter, with four yellow pansies that crouched close together in the dry soil.

Above the wall of the yard, Malik could see the other cottages and, above them, the dark blue funnel of the ship. To the right of the funnel was another building that he hadn't noticed last night – a ware-house that must be on the quayside, with bright red wooden doors for windows. A groan of engines came from the dock behind it. Perhaps Hector and Vex had already left for the dock?

Malik went to the back gate and opened the latch. He stepped into the alley and looked both ways. What had seemed so frightening last night had now become the most ordinary place in the world. He heard a rustle, looked down and saw a cat tug at the head of a fish that poked from a rusted hole in the upturned rubbish bin they had stumbled on last night. Malik knelt and watched the cat, but when it sensed him it let go of the fish and retreated, its body crouched and tense. It was a hairball of a cat, black with a white sock on each paw and a triangle of white under its chin that reminded Malik of Papa's beard.

He stretched out his hand and rubbed his fingers together. He made the smooching noise that cats couldn't resist and the cat, which looked only just old enough to fend for itself, stretched out its neck and sniffed, but it wouldn't come closer.

Malik took three careful steps and knelt by the bin. The fish head smelled bad. He waved away some flies and prodded it. The flesh was soft and the dead eye looked like a dirty puddle. He put his finger in behind the head and flipped it out of the hole so that it skidded across the alleyway and stopped at the cat's feet. It prodded it and turned it over, pausing only to look at Malik suspiciously.

Malik stayed very still as the cat began to eat. Papa had told him that you should never approach an animal that is hurt or hungry, and when they had been with the dying dog in the cellar, Papa had let him throw a piece of ham close to its head, but he hadn't let Malik go any nearer than that.

So Malik waited.

When the cat had finished eating it came to him itself and allowed him to stroke the fur along its arched back. It purred and nudged its nose into his hand. Malik tickled it under the belly as the cat walked to and fro, rubbing itself against his bare legs and the top of his Wellington boots.

Malik picked the cat up and it didn't seem to mind. He thought it was probably thirsty, so he carried it into the kitchen, and because he had no bowl he poured a little water into the bucket and left it on its side. The cat stretched itself and sniffed. It took a lick of the water and once it knew it was fresh, it began to drink with quick laps of its tiny pink tongue.

'Malik!' Papa shouted from upstairs. 'Hector? Vex? Is anyone there?'

'I'm here, Papa.' Malik ran out into the hall.

Papa stood at the top of the staircase. His face was white and haunted and the pockets of his trousers were turned inside out. 'Where is Hector? Where is Vex? Are they with you in the kitchen?'

Malik shook his head. 'They're not here, Papa. They have gone out already and they left the door unlocked.'

Papa stood in the centre of the room holding his winter coat. He had a hand deep in one of the pockets. He brought out his passport and dropped it onto the mattress where his keys and wallet already lay. He turned the coat around and felt the outside pockets, first the left and then the right, his forehead creasing into deep furrows, his hands worried and frantic. He produced the two red apples and dropped them on the floor without a second glance. Malik watched them roll across the boards and settle under the window – he knew they weren't what Papa was searching for.

Papa was muttering. He talked to himself in fast, clipped sentences that Malik could barely understand. Then he dropped the coat at his feet and his hand went suddenly to his heart and a finger scooped inside the small pocket on the left breast of his shirt, but it was empty like the others.

He touched his face. Felt his jaw and winced. He looked around the room, bewildered, took in the upturned chair and the wardrobe as though he had never seen them. Then he sucked saliva back into the side of his mouth that wouldn't close properly, and his eyes darted from one end of the room to the other. He began to shake, his shoulders shivering and his head beginning to twitch. His mouth fell open.

Malik thought Papa would collapse he was so unsteady on his feet, and when he began to bend at the middle, Malik took a step forward, but Papa regained some control of his body and Malik stepped away again, scared to get too close.

Papa seemed to not even know he was there. He reached down, picked up his coat and felt again in every pocket, trying to be calm, but all the while he was frantic and muttering, with hands that moved too quickly so that he dropped the coat on the floor.

He left it where it lay, stepped around it and stood on the collar. He gripped the edge of the inner pocket, then pulled hard, tearing the lining from the inside of the jacket in one long strip of red silk that remained attached at the hem. He turned the coat around and did the same on the other side, then shook it vigorously, turned it upside down and shook again. When nothing fell out, he threw it at the wardrobe.

'No!' Papa shouted. 'No. No. No.'

Malik moved from foot to foot and his hand held the front of his blue shorts. He had never seen Papa look like this and he didn't know what he could do to make it any better.

Papa stood still, his lips pursed, staring blankly out of the window.

Malik waited.

Finally Papa said what they both knew. 'They have robbed me.'

The two of them said nothing after that. They simply stood there until the cat walked into the bedroom and sauntered across the floorboards toward the window. It rubbed itself against Papa's ankle and he kicked it hard with his heel, sending the creature skidding into the corner with a screech of a howl.

'Stop it!' shouted Malik. 'Stop it!'

He ran to the cat but it dodged him, skittered across the floor and ran back out of the door. Malik let it go. He circled Papa at a distance as Papa clenched his fists into tight balls that he put to the temples of his head. He bent over till his elbows touched his hips and he sat down heavily on the wooden chair, put his head between his knees and moaned.

Malik stood back at a safe distance. He waited until Papa had stopped moaning and then he asked, 'Papa? Are you all right?' He took a step closer. 'Papa?'

Papa kept his head bowed and Malik didn't know whether he should ask again or say nothing. Papa spoke to the floor. 'My face hurts.'

Malik couldn't think what to do about that. He said, 'Mama will be here soon. She'll know what to do, Papa. I know she will.'

Papa looked up quickly. He pointed a finger at Malik. '*I* know what to do! Do you think *I* don't know what to do?'

Malik stepped back and his hand went to the front of his shorts again. Papa lowered his head and stared at the floor. 'Can I use the toilet?' Malik took his hand away in case Papa saw, but when Papa didn't look up he went to the bathroom anyway. He left the door open wide enough so that he could see the pipe in the floor and his wee fell in a golden arc that spattered on the side of the pipe, then fell away into darkness.

When Malik came back into the room, Papa was still in the chair with his head bowed. Malik waited to be noticed, but when it didn't happen he said, 'Perhaps the diamond doesn't matter, Papa.' He sounded uncertain. He looked down at the wallet on the mattress, still thick with banknotes. 'You still have all that money.'

Papa touched the side of his face where it had swollen. 'You're right.' He spoke quietly and his eyes were grim. 'Yes, you're right. Perhaps it doesn't matter. It's only money. It's the betrayal that matters. That's what hurts more.' Papa looked Malik in the eye. 'The diamond would have made everything easier. That's all. Everything would have been that much simpler for us. You're too young to realize, but it would.'

The sound of a motor came from the street outside. Malik ran across to the window in time to see a vehicle drive past the cottage, and it wasn't a soldier's jeep but a civilian car with shining black paint and polished chrome. Its wheels rattled on the cobblestones.

Papa arrived beside Malik as the tail lights

rounded the corner. He turned the pockets of his trousers back the right way and hurried over to the mattress. 'People are arriving at the port. I must be quick.'

Malik didn't know whether this was good or bad but it felt important.

Papa picked up his keys and passport, and the wallet with the cash, and he stuffed them in his trouser pockets. He went over to the wardrobe, took his coat from the floor and shook it out. He leaned inside the wardrobe door, found the knife that he had left in there from the previous night, opened out the blade and cut away the strip of red silk that he had torn from the lining of his coat, making it wearable again.

'Where are we going?' asked Malik.

Papa picked up the rucksack and searched in the pockets. '*You're* not going anywhere. *I* have to go to the docks but I won't be long.'

'I want to come with you.'

'It's better that you stay here.'

Malik's chest tightened. 'But I don't want to be on my own. It's not safe.'

'It will be, and anyway, I won't be long.'

'What if Mama is at the docks?'

Papa took a black leather notebook and a silver pen from the rucksack. He stuffed them into the pocket of his coat. 'She won't be.'

'But what if she is? She should be here today. You said we would meet her at the ship when it sailed and that was meant to be today.' Malik was desperate. 'She might already be there.'

Papa was impatient. 'She'll know it's been delayed. She won't expect us to be there, and anyway, if I see her I can bring her back with me.'

Malik knew the only way to persuade Papa was with logic, like he had with the torch in the alley. He tried not to speak until he was sure that he had something worth saying. 'But you said I was good at looking. You told me we make a good team. It would be better if there were two of us. We could make a better job of looking for her.'

'No, Malik. It's better that you stay here.' Papa didn't even bother to give a reason.

Malik stamped his foot. 'But I don't want to be on my own. What if someone comes here?'

'They won't come.'

'But what if they do? They did last night!'

'Aaaaghh . . .' Papa put a hand to his forehead. 'That's too many questions. Just like yesterday. For heaven's sake, I have only just woken up. I haven't even had a chance to start counting and I still think you've bust your limit.'

'I don't care!' Malik burst into tears. 'I don't care about your stupid counting.'

There! He had said it. He stared defiantly and Papa met his gaze and they stood with both their eyes burning. Malik didn't care if Papa got angry and he didn't care that he was crying.

Papa blinked first. He lifted the rucksack from the floor, looked inside it for nothing in particular and then put it back down. 'Go ahead and cry.' His voice was gentle when he met Malik's eye. 'You deserve a good cry. Really. I mean it. You have been very brave these past few days, Malik.' Papa reached out and touched his arm. 'I sometimes forget how old you are. I'm sorry.'

Malik immediately felt bad. He was ashamed of himself and he could hear from the tone of Papa's voice that he wasn't going to give in – he was still going to convince Malik to stay in the cottage.

Papa was quiet and assured. 'We do make a good team. We wouldn't have got this far if we didn't make a good team.'

Malik waited for the 'but'.

Papa squeezed his shoulder. 'But every team needs a leader. That's right, isn't it? And anything that's worth doing involves moments when we have to do things we don't want to do. I've said that before, haven't I?' Malik let his head drop but Papa lifted his chin with one finger. 'Right now, I need you to stay here in this house. I don't want you to go outside. I want you to stay right here in this room until I get back, OK? I will try not to be long but if you stay inside then you'll be safe. Do you understand?'

'What if the soldiers come and take me away?'

'I don't think the soldiers will take you away, Malik. I really don't.'

Malik shrugged his shoulders.

'We all choose who to trust, Malik. Sometimes we get it wrong like I did last night, but you can always trust me. Do you understand? You can trust me to put you first before anything else.'

Malik shuffled his feet. 'I haven't got anything to do. I'll be bored.'

'You have your magic trick. That takes lots of practice.'

'I don't have a coin.'

Papa brought out his wallet and took a coin from the little pocket on the inside. He handed it to Malik and closed his hand round it. 'I want to see a clean French Drop when I get back.' Papa picked up an apple from the floor and touched the place where it had bruised. 'Have these apples if you get hungry, but try not to start on the bread and tuna in the rucksack before I'm back.'

Papa walked quickly out of the door and down the stairs and Malik heard the creak of the hinges as the back door shut. He turned the coin over in his fingers, tried to palm it like Papa did, and watched the coin drop to the floor.

Papa pushed at the bright red door of the Port Authority building. It opened the length of an arm before a man moved across the doorway.

'You here for the ship?' he asked Papa.

'Yes. I wanted to speak –'

'You should ask downstairs.'

Papa leaned in toward the closing gap. 'I know that. I wanted to speak with Nicholas Massa –'

The door was closed before he had finished what he wanted to say. Papa stared at the glossy red paint, then knocked and waited, and when nothing happened he knocked again. The door opened wide enough to show an eye, a mouth and the rim of a dark brown hat. 'Go away,' said the man.

Behind Papa's back there were hollow voices in the tall brick hallway and feet coming up the stairs. Papa turned to see a group of four men, and in the middle of them was Nicholas Massa – Papa knew his face from photographs. He stepped forward to meet them, said 'Excuse me, sir,' but one of the other men reached him first and eased him away from the top of the stairs. Massa walked past, intending not to stop.

Papa shouted out. 'I'm a friend of Angelo Vex.'

Massa stopped walking and turned to look at Papa. The skin on his face was tight and smooth except for a crow's foot at the edge of each eye and it seemed he only smiled at cameras.

'He spoke of you only last night,' Papa added quickly.

The party of men paused and Massa stepped through them and came closer. 'You know Angelo Vex? I assume you want a ticket for the ship?'

'I want two tickets.'

'I bet you do. They're not cheap.'

Papa nodded. 'Ten thousand each, I heard.'

Massa shook his head. 'Fifteen thousand. Paid in cash.' He made no apology for looking Papa up and down. 'Do you have the money?'

Papa kept his eyes steady. He didn't want Massa to see anything but certainty. 'There's something else. My daughter, Maria. I need to find her.'

Massa waved a hand as though there were flies about his head. 'I cannot help you – that has nothing to do with me.' He moved toward the door and the other men closed around him.

'I could be of help to you.' Papa walked quickly along beside them as they approached the red door. He had to walk on his tip-toes to see above the shoulders of the men. 'I may have something that you want.'

Nicholas Massa stopped at the bright red door. He turned to Papa, an eyebrow raised in disbelief. 'And what could a man like you possibly have that I might want?'

Malik took out his penknife and opened all the tools. He had a metal shape that opened bottle tops and a corkscrew. He had a file and a toothpick. He closed them again so that only the knife blade remained, then he picked up one of the apples, cut it in half and cut each half into thirds. He lined the apple segments up in a row along the floorboard at his feet, making sure to keep the bruised piece in the middle.

The cat appeared cautiously at the door. Malik let it choose to come in and when it did, it walked over and put its nose to each of the apple pieces. 'Eat them if you want to,' Malik told it but the cat didn't want to. Malik ate the pieces himself, and when he was finished he slid the plastic toothpick from its slot in the penknife and picked at the bits of apple that were stuck between his teeth.

The cat pounced on the strip of red silk that lay on the floor, turning it up around its head and Malik held the other end and got the cat to jump around the room and hang onto it with its claws.

The sound of an engine made Malik drop the silk. This was louder than before, a deep throb that shook the window in its frame. Something was coming down the street, and it was bigger than a car and there were boots running on the cobblestones. A man shouted, 'Bring them on. Bring it this way.'

Malik took three quick steps to the window. There were soldiers in the street! He drew back so he wouldn't be seen. He should hide. He looked for the cat but found it was no longer in the room and he ran to the top of the stairs and saw its tail disappear into the living room. The house was full of the sound of engines and boots. Malik went halfway down the stairs. 'Come here, cat,' he whispered, but when the cat didn't appear he went on past the front door and looked into the room.

The cat stood up on the windowsill, sniffing the fresh air through the broken window. There were soldiers in the street right outside now. Malik smooched his lips and rustled his fingers, but the cat didn't budge until the side of a tank drew across the front of the cottage, close enough that the view of the street became one large block of grey metal that came to a standstill and shuddered like a nervous animal. A line of rivets shivered in the holes across its flank. The brakes let out a gasp of air, which made the cat leap from the window and run back across the room. Malik bent down and scooped it up as it tried to pass him through the doorway.

'Keep them coming!' shouted a voice that was close. 'Keep them coming through.'

Malik heard a footstep behind him. He turned to see a man standing in the porch, just the other side of the frosted glass panels in the front door. There was the click of a lighter and Malik saw a flame and the fierce orange dot of a cigarette that faded when the man took it from his mouth. If the soldier were to crouch down now and look through the letterbox, he would see Malik standing there holding the cat, staring at him as though he were a ghost.

Malik thought about running. He looked back up the staircase but he dare not move, dare not even flinch, as the man smoked his cigarette and the convoy went on past the cottage. Malik looked back into the living room. The tank was still outside, level with the window – he could even smell the fumes from the exhaust. Then quite suddenly the tank jerked back to life. The engine roared and the joints groaned and the line of rivets began to move across the window until the tank was gone and Malik could see the street again, full of jeeps and armoured cars and soldiers that passed the cottage on their way toward the dock.

Malik knew these soldiers weren't like the ones that he'd seen from the cellar or at the roadblocks. These soldiers had neat uniforms, all identical with proper metal helmets. The soldiers Malik had seen before, in town, had all been dressed differently from each other and most of them hadn't looked like soldiers at all. Some had worn army fatigues, but they'd had their own jackets over the top or they had tied bright sashes around their heads as though they thought they were kings. Papa had said they weren't soldiers at all – he'd said they were a ragtag outfit of thugs and chancers, dressed in clothes they had taken from the dead.

Perhaps these soldiers in the street were the peacekeepers that Hector had talked about and they had come to make the port safe?

Malik held the cat tightly and stayed where he was until the soldier at the front door threw down his cigarette and was gone. The sound of engines and feet faded down the cobbled street and away toward the port.

Malik slouched against the stairs and took a deep breath. But then he realized there were still people outside in the street. He became alert. He could hear voices and see outlines of passing figures through the frosted glass. He peered into the living room and could see men, women and children walking past the broken window, both on the pavement and down the middle of the cobbled street. They carried hold-alls and suitcases and they wore their heavy winter coats just like Papa. Malik hadn't seen people out in the open like this since the day before the soldiers had taken Mama, and that must mean that something had changed, that it was safe to be in the street again.

Malik went and stood at the shattered glass – there were so many people that it didn't seem to matter if he was seen there now. He watched a man wrestle his way across the cobblestones with a large trunk on a trolley, and he caught the eye of a young girl being carried on the shoulder of her father, who saw the cat in his arms and pointed at him, smiling.

Malik suddenly thought that Mama might be in amongst these people. She might even be there in the street right now. He began to search the faces of the women, quickly moving from one to the next, and he looked for the hem of a blue dress beneath the winter coats, but there were too many people, too many faces for him to be certain that he had seen them all.

It would be easier if he went outside. He ran to the front door, pulled at the latch and stepped onto the pavement. He left the front door wide open behind him and stood in the middle of the street so he could see the faces of everyone walking toward him. There was a woman holding a cage with a songbird but this woman was clearly not his mother. There was a couple who struggled with two bags each, and she stopped to put one down and the man told her to 'Hurry up'. Malik stepped to one side so he could see behind them.

He began to move with the crowd along the street, past the bombed-out houses on the opposite pavement, where a woman stopped to smack her child behind the knees. He passed the locked doors of the empty houses, weaving between the luggage and the legs of people, looking for a sign that his mother might be there, and as he walked the rims of his Wellington boots smacked against his bare shins and the dark blue funnel of the ship came closer.

At the last cottage, the road turned right and opened out to become the quayside. There was a chain-link fence and a tall metal gate across the entrance to the docks. A jeep stood there with its engine running, two soldiers sitting in the front seats, smoking cigarettes and watching the crowd come through. Just inside the fence was the charred wreckage of a small light aircraft that was tilted uneasily to one side with the tip of one wing touching the ground.

Malik slowed his pace to look at the plane and

the corner of a woman's suitcase caught the back of his head hard enough that it hurt. 'Keep up,' she scolded him. 'Keep up or get out of the way.'

Malik stepped aside and the cat shifted its position on his shoulder and its claws scratched at the skin beneath his shirt. He didn't dare go further in case the soldiers wouldn't allow him back. Behind him there was only a straggle of people left in the street and his mother wasn't amongst them, so he walked back to the cottages, hugging the cat to his chest.

When he reached the cottage door he found it closed. He pushed, and when it didn't open he went to the window and looked into the empty living room. There was no sign of anyone so he decided to try the back door and he ran to the top end of the street, turned the corner into the alley and ran along, tapping each gate till he came to the thirteenth cottage.

At the back door he hesitated. What if someone had come in from the street and was now inside the house? He put his face to the kitchen window. He could see the tap. He could see through the hall to the front door. There was no one inside. He opened the back door, listened, then crept along into the hall.

Papa's voice came from the upstairs room. 'Who's down there?'

Malik was relieved. 'Papa? Papa? Is that you?'

'Come upstairs, Malik,' Papa shouted down.

Malik walked up the wooden stairs and stopped at the bedroom door. He saw the back of a man sitting in the chair, with Papa standing over him. Malik stepped inside and circled the room, saw the face of Hector Valentine, and under his chin saw the blade of Papa's knife.

'Where have you been?' Papa addressed Malik, but kept his eyes on Hector. 'I told you to stay here.'

'Let me go, Salvatore,' Hector pleaded. 'I told you –'

Papa nudged the knife upwards, cutting the sentence short. 'Shut up. You've told me nothing.' Papa flicked a finger at Malik. 'I asked: where have you been?'

Malik held the cat close to his face for comfort. 'I followed all the people heading to the docks, Papa. I thought I might find Mama.'

Papa tutted. 'I asked you not to go outside. Didn't I say that? You should do as I tell you, Malik. I don't tell you to do something without a reason. Always remember that.'

Hector turned his face to Malik. 'Tell your grandad to let me go, Malik, eh? He's got it all wrong. It wasn't me. I didn't steal the diamond. It was *Vex*. Vex did it and I tried –' Papa made a quick little jab of the knife at Hector's face, making him scream out in pain. 'Aaargh!'

Malik put a hand up to his own mouth.

'For God's sake, Salvatore.' Hector touched the blood that had begun to trickle down his chin. 'You cut me.'

'You're lying!' Papa shook the knife in his face. 'If you had tried to stop Vex, I would have woken up. I would have heard you.'

'It happened outside . . .'

'If it happened outside you would have come back and woken me straightaway. Only you didn't, did you? Did you fight him? No? I didn't think so. You're lying to me. I can tell.' Papa moved his lips as though he had a bad taste in his mouth and was about to spit. 'I always know when you lie to me, Hector. I have an instinct for it. Like when you told me I should put my money into those Ligurian bonds. Do you remember? I knew then you were lying, and I know it now. So tell me the truth. You both stole the diamond, didn't you? The two of you went through my pockets like thieves in the night, eh? That's the truth, isn't it?'

Hector stretched out a hand toward Malik. The blood from his face was smeared across a single finger. 'Malik, for God's sake, make him stop.'

Malik could see the bite mark that Papa had made the night before. 'Stop it, Papa,' he said. 'Please.'

Papa saw the bite too and he slapped Hector's face with his free hand.

'Hey!' Hector shouted. 'Stop this, you old fool. Enough, huh? That's enough!'

Papa put the knife back at Hector's throat. His hand was shaking. 'You think I won't do it? You think I'm too old? Is that it? Too scared of you? Well, I'm not scared of you, you little man. Now, tell me where he is.'

Hector flexed his hands and sighed. He put his head right back to look at the ceiling. 'This is so stupid.' He put his hands in the air as if to surrender. 'OK, OK, I'll tell you. It doesn't matter now anyway – we've both lost. Just put that thing away, Salvatore, eh? Put the knife down and let me talk to you, man to man. You don't need the knife.'

Papa stepped back and held the knife by his side.

Hector took a handkerchief from his trouser pocket and dabbed at the wound on his face. He flicked the wedge of hair away from his eyes. 'The truth is, I don't know where they are. Not Vex and not the diamond. He tricked me too. I saw him take the jewel from you and I followed him downstairs and confronted him. He said I should come with him.'

'I knew it . . .'

'He promised me half the money when we sold it, and I went along with it, yes, but then he gave me the slip. He disappeared with the diamond and I don't know where he is. I was looking for him when you found me first. That's the truth of it. Really, it is.' Hector shook his head. 'We've both been robbed.'

Papa shook the knife in Hector's face again. 'You've not been robbed! How could you have been robbed? The diamond was never yours.' Papa put the point of the knife under Hector's eye. 'Do you know what it feels like to have a friend steal from you? Do you? Can you imagine it? The humiliation? I should gouge your eyes out. I should slit your throat.'

'Don't do it, Papa.' Malik began to cry. 'Please. I don't like it.' The cat wriggled free from his arms, fell to the floor and ran toward the wardrobe.

But Hector stayed calm. He put a finger up to the knife and gently moved it from his face. He turned to Malik. 'Everything's all right, Malik. Don't get upset.' He looked up at Papa. 'See what you're doing to him? Put the knife away, man! You're upsetting him. Isn't it bad enough that his mother is missing? You do know where they're taking the women, don't you? They're going to the big hotel at the back of the town. They're taking as many as they can find and they're not coming back. You know it as well as I do. You should be out looking for your daughter, not worrying about getting revenge. The diamond's gone, man. Long gone. And that's a fact.'

Malik felt like he'd been cut. He put a hand to his chest and pressed where it hurt. What did Hector mean about Mama?

Papa stepped back and lowered the knife and Hector shook his head as though he pitied the old man. 'Your grandfather won't slit my throat, Malik.' He sat up straight in his chair and checked his handkerchief to see if he had stopped bleeding. 'You won't, will you, Salvatore? After all, we're not killers, you and I. We're respectable people. We're businessmen. We don't go around pulling knives on people. At least, we don't if there's nothing to be gained from it.

And Salvatore, if you're honest, you know that you would have done the same as I did.'

'I would not.'

'Yes, you would. If the tables were turned. Perhaps if you were younger, for sure.'

'I was going to share the money.' Papa's voice was quieter. 'Don't you remember? I intended to buy tickets for us all.'

'Only because you thought you needed us. You realized you couldn't do it by yourself and you wanted Vex to smooth things over.'

Malik wanted Papa to just let Hector go. He didn't care who had stolen the diamond – it wasn't important. But he did want to know if Hector knew where Mama was. That *was* important.

Hector shrugged as though there was nothing more he could do. 'It's business after all, isn't it, Salvatore? It's money. The winner takes all. The way it's always been. That's the game we've all played, and the truth of it is that Vex was always better playing the game than either of us.'

'That's not true.'

Hector got to his feet and Papa made no move to stop him. 'Yes, it is. It's been true for all of us – it's how it has always been. We didn't worry about the losers when we were winning. There's no point in complaining about it now.' He walked over to the door.

'Where are you going?'

Hector shrugged. 'Does it matter?'

Papa lifted his knife again. He took a step toward Hector. 'Give me your wallet.'

'What?'

'Give me your wallet.' Papa shook the knife and stepped closer. 'I mean it. I want you to know what it feels like to be robbed by a friend. I want you to have nothing left.'

Hector actually laughed. He shook his head but he took out his wallet, opened it and removed the cash that had been with him from the night before. He counted out three notes from the top and threw the remaining bills onto the floorboards so that they spread across the room. He held up the three notes. 'I would like to keep the price of a melon, if that's all the same to you.' He put the three notes back into his wallet and put the wallet in his trouser pocket. 'You can have the rest, Salvatore. But remember, we were never friends. It was always business. I thought you understood that.' He nodded to Malik on his way out of the room.

Papa folded the blade of the knife back into the handle and put it away in his trouser pocket. He looked defeated. He ran the palm of his hand across his face, then bent down on one knee and began to pick up the banknotes from the floorboards. 'Don't stand there doing nothing, you silly boy. Give me a hand. All this crouching down's no good for me.'

Malik knelt beside him to pick up the notes. He put the large pink ones at the back of his hand the same way Papa did and the cat rubbed itself against their ankles as they crawled across the floor.

He wanted to ask about Mama but now wasn't the right time – it would only provoke Papa. And yet the question was there and it wouldn't go away.

'You seem to have a friend.' Papa nodded down at the cat. 'Does it have a name?'

Malik shook his head.

'You should name it yourself.'

'It must have one already but I don't know what it is.'

'That's true.' Papa picked up the last banknote and rested with an arm across his knee. 'I'm sorry I kicked it earlier. I was upset. I shouldn't have done it.'

'No,' Malik said bitterly. 'You shouldn't.'

'Well, I'm sorry.'

Malik ignored Papa's apology. He put his own pile of notes on the floor and Papa took them and shuffled them together with the ones in his hand. He held the money out to Malik. 'Take this. You should have it.'

Malik shook his head. He didn't want Hector's money. 'Why did Hector say Mama was taken to a hotel?' There. He had asked it.

Papa looked away. 'I don't know. It's something he made up. I don't know why he said that.'

Malik knew that Papa was lying to him. He raised his voice. 'I want to go back and look for her, Papa. I want to go to the hotel.'

'No, Malik, you can't do that. We have to catch the ship.' Papa nudged the money into Malik's chest. 'Please, take the money.'

Malik ignored the cash. He stood up. 'I'm going to find the hotel. Which one did Hector mean?'

Papa stood up too. 'Hector doesn't know what he's talking about!' he shouted.

'Then why did he say that she was at the big hotel?'

'I don't know. Hector thinks he knows everything but he doesn't. He can't do, because I saw her today. OK? Are you satisfied?'

Malik's heart leaped into his mouth. He stepped quickly across to Papa and stood close so they couldn't avoid each other's eyes.

'Where did you see her? Was she at the docks?'

'Yes. I saw her at the docks.'

'But . . . where? She wasn't with those people in the street. I looked for her everywhere and I couldn't find her.'

'No. She wasn't with those people. She was at the docks before then. I saw her before I found Hector, before I put my knife to that thieving bastard's throat and brought him here. I saw her, Malik, and I spoke to her. So you don't need to worry. She is fine. She is safe and she will be at the docks tomorrow. That's what she told me.'

Malik wanted to believe Papa – he really did – but he couldn't tell whether he was lying or not and anyway, he couldn't think straight. The idea that Mama could have been so close but was not here with him now was more than he could bear. 'So where is she?' he howled. 'Where is she now?' He looked quickly over to the door, in case she might be standing there. 'If she knew I was here she would come and find me. I know she would.'

'Are you calling me a liar?' Papa shouted in

Malik's face. 'Is that what you think of me? Is it?'

Malik pulled away and threw himself down on the mattress in tears.

Papa came and stood over him. He put his hands into his pockets and then took them out again. 'She's my daughter,' he said quietly. 'Don't forget that, Malik. Mama means the same to me as you do to her. Just because she's older doesn't make it any different. I wouldn't lie about my own daughter.'

Malik didn't want to listen but he heard what Papa said and it made sense. But why hadn't she come back with Papa? Where was she? Malik knew better than to ask more questions, so he just put his head on his knees and cried.

Papa fiddled with his fingers. 'Stop that, eh?' He leaned down and put a hand to Malik's head. 'Come on. Come on.' Malik let Papa wipe the tears from the top of his cheeks. 'You're a very brave boy, Malik. Very brave. It's not right what you have had to put up with. It's not right at all. Mama has so much to do before the ship leaves, but she told me to tell you that she loves you very much. She asked me if you were being brave and I told her you were. I said we make a good team.'

That sounded like just the sort of thing that

Mama would say and Malik wanted to believe it. He really wanted to. He lifted his head. 'When did Mama say she would meet us?'

'At ten o'clock, Malik. She said she would meet us at ten o'clock.'

'At the front of the building with the red windows?'

The old man threw his hands in the air. 'Still so many questions! Yes, at the front of the warehouse. At the place where anyone would meet their loved ones. Is there anywhere else to meet at the docks? Because I can't think of anywhere.'

'At the big crane. That would be a good place to meet.'

'The big crane? Well, yes, I suppose so. But it's not at the crane. We shall meet at the warehouse, right by the big red front door. That's what we agreed. Tomorrow morning at ten o'clock.'

Malik had a place and a time. So that was definite. That was for sure. He flung his arms round Papa's neck and kissed his bruised face gently. 'I'm sorry I was rude, Papa.'

Papa smiled. He looked pleased and a little embarrassed. He pulled away from Malik and stood up. 'Now you must stop asking all these questions because I must think things through.' He brushed his trousers down with the back of his hand. 'Young people ask too many questions. Have I ever told you that? No one does as they're told any more. When I was your age, I wouldn't dream of asking so many questions. I wouldn't have dared!' He reached into his jacket pocket and brought out a paper bag full of chestnuts. 'Shame these have gone cold. There was a man with a brazier at the dock.' Papa took a chestnut for himself, then handed the bag to Malik who took one of the cracked brown nuts and loosened the skin with his knife.

Papa let the peeled skin drop to the floor. 'They weren't as cheap as they could have been, but he was doing good business. He'll be busy till the ship leaves.'

Malik chewed on the soft brown nut and thought of the candied chestnuts they would eat at Christmas. These tasted just as good.

Papa put the chestnut into his mouth and winced as he chewed. 'Hey, did I tell you that I saw the name on our ship? It's called the *Samaritan*. It's written across the back of the ship in big white letters. It's a good name for a ship, don't you think?'

'The Good Samaritan.'

'No, just the *Samaritan*.'

'It should be the Good Samaritan. Like it is in the story.'

Papa weighed it up. 'I suppose it should. Even so, it's still a good name for a ship. They won't turn people away. Not with a name like that written across the back in large white letters.'

Malik thought about the ship at the dock. 'Do you know where it will take us?' he asked. 'Have you been there before?'

Papa nodded. 'I have been there once. Yes. Only for a short visit. It's a big country. Plenty of room for everyone. Plenty of space to stretch your legs. The people who live there like to say yes. They like new ideas and they like people who get things done. I think we'll be very welcome.'

'And will we have a nice place to live?'

'I hope so. They have lovely houses. They're big, but not too expensive.' Papa leaned forward. 'All the houses are made of white painted wood and every house has a front garden with a white picket fence and another garden at the back. They have big gardens there because they have lots of land. In fact, they're so big that each house has a post box on a pole at the front gate so that the postman doesn't have to walk all the way to the front door. It's a good idea, isn't it? Because, I'm telling you, those gardens aren't small.'

'So he leaves your letters in a box at the front gate?'

'Yes he does.'

'And people don't steal them?'

'No, they don't. That's a good point. I hadn't thought of that but you're right – they could steal them if they wanted to but they don't, so that makes me think it must be a country where people trust one another. It'll be a new experience to live in a place that's honest, eh?'

Malik thought about the pretty wooden houses with the white fences and the post boxes on poles. Mama would probably give him the job of fetching the post in the morning. That's just the sort of thing she would do and he wouldn't mind a bit. He stopped himself from dreaming. 'But we don't have the money for a ticket so how will we get on the ship?' he worried.

Papa's eyes gleamed. 'Don't you worry, Malik. We'll be on that ship tomorrow. I met with the man at the dock and we have reached an understanding. He knows me and I know him.' Papa touched the side of his nose. 'We have done a deal, Malik. We've shaken hands. There's no way that ship is leaving without us.'

The arc lamp on the quayside lit up at twilight, exposing the ship against the darkening sky above the cottages. The people waiting at the dock knew that the ship wouldn't leave today so some of them drifted away in search of shelter.

Malik and Papa watched from the upstairs window as the people came along the street. The women put their faces to the glass of the downstairs windows and the men put their shoulders to the doors to see if they would open. Some of their faces were lit by hand-held torches or little nightlight candles that flickered from jam jars that they held up in front of them.

Papa brought the candle up to the windowsill of the bedroom so that people knew the house was occupied. In the cottage opposite their own, a man tried the door, found it opened and ushered his wife and children inside.

Malik took Papa's hand. 'Are these the people from this morning?'

'I expect most of them are.' Papa looked down at the pavement where a couple had stopped outside their cottage and were looking up at them. Their only luggage was a baby wrapped in a blanket. 'Just one minute,' said Papa, and he hurried from the room. Malik heard the front door open, saw the couple step towards the hall, and heard their voices from the room below.

'I have given them the downstairs room,' Papa told Malik when he came back upstairs. 'Better to have a full house, and I don't think they will trouble us. Let's have something to eat.'

Papa brought his rucksack over to the mattress and they sat down next to each other. Papa halved the loaf of bread and opened the tin of tuna. He scooped out flakes of the fish with his knife. 'Don't give any to the cat,' he told Malik. 'There isn't enough.'

But Malik couldn't resist the cat's longing eyes so he let a piece fall onto the floor as soon as Papa looked away.

When they had finished eating there were a lot more people out in the street.

'We don't need to be frightened.' Papa watched them from the window. 'We should go and meet them. There may be people out there who know more than us.'

They went downstairs and stood at the open front door, nodding to the people in the street. Papa was a good talker. He smiled and said 'Hello.' He shook hands, laughed and slapped people on the back as if he had known them all his life. Malik liked Papa being so relaxed – it made him feel safe.

When a man offered them food, Papa went off down the street with him, telling Malik to stay by the door. Papa returned later with three bananas, eight segments of chocolate and a small slab of cheese wrapped in brown paper. He had also found three tins of cat food and an old metal saucepan. They went back upstairs and he laid everything out along the floor, the same way he had done with the contents of the rucksack when they had first arrived.

'No one could tell me anything that I didn't already know,' Papa told Malik. 'The ship will leave tomorrow just as I said. The troops have been sent to keep the peace around the port and ensure the ship leaves without any incident. We'll be safe here tonight.' He pulled the lid from a small flat tin and handed the cat food to Malik. 'We should save the rest of the food for tomorrow. Is that all right with you or are you still hungry?'

Malik broke the cat food into pieces with his penknife. 'No, I'm fine. Thank you.' He put the tin on the floor for the cat to sniff.

Papa gave Malik a straight look. 'Do you want to use the toilet before bed? I don't want you using the bathroom in the night. Not now there are other people in the house.' He put the saucepan down by the mattress. 'You can use this if you need to go in the night.'

Malik knew there was no way he was going to use the saucepan. 'I don't want to. I'll be fine.'

'Are you ready to sleep?'

Malik shrugged. He wasn't ready to sleep. 'You haven't shown me the magic trick today.'

'You haven't practised. There's no point in me showing you if you don't practise.' Papa was smiling. He showed Malik the coin in his fingers, then held it up close to Malik's eyes. 'Sleight of hand,' Papa said. 'This is how you do the French Drop. I make your eyes watch what I want you to watch . . .' He flourished his free hand toward the coin in his fingers. 'And the coin disappears.'

Malik touched where the coin had been, all the

time knowing it was in the hand that Papa stretched out toward his collar. He caught Papa's other hand, opened it out and saw the coin palmed at the base of his thumb. Papa closed his hand up, reached behind Malik's ear and produced the coin in his fingers.

'There's no such thing as magic, Malik. Just trickery and the practice it takes to pull it off.'

Malik took hold of the coin. He flourished it, held it up, then made the switch. The coin dropped onto the floor at his feet. He ran, picked it up and tried again, only for the coin to drop as before. 'I can't do it, Papa. It's too difficult.'

'You can do it. It took me two days of practice and it will take you the same.' Papa put his hand out for the coin and pocketed it. 'Perhaps you will learn more quickly than I did. You're a bright boy. Now settle down and get some sleep.'

Malik lay down on the mattress and pulled his jacket up across his shoulders. He watched Papa settle himself on the floor by the door, so that he would be woken if anyone came in the room. He saw Papa wince when he pressed his hip against the wooden boards, and again when he put his cheek to the rucksack, which he used as a pillow. Papa turned onto his back and closed his eyes. He was asleep before Malik.

Malik couldn't sleep, despite being tired. He lay awake imagining what it would be like tomorrow, meeting Mama at the dock and going on the tall ship with all these other people. He had that fidgety feeling in his stomach that meant he was excited.

Or scared. One or the other, it was difficult to know which.

In the morning, Malik woke first. He stood over Papa and watched him sleep. The bruising had spread across Papa's cheek so that it looked like a map, deep patches of purple and red with a pale yellow outline that had seeped into the socket of his eye.

Malik didn't want to be late for the ship. He shook his grandfather awake. 'Papa! Papa!'

Papa groaned and rolled onto his side. 'What time is it? It must be too early to get up.' He opened one eye slowly and then the other. 'I never seem to get to sleep until the moment before you wake me. Why is that?'

'You've been snoring,' said Malik.

Papa put his weight onto one elbow with a moan. 'I have aches where I didn't think I had bones.' He caught his breath, pulled his knees up to his chest and rolled over onto his front, took another breath then pulled himself into a sitting position, his knees still folded up beneath him. 'If I wanted to do yoga I would have had some lessons by now, don't you think?' He stretched his arms out in front of him. 'And I don't snore. Please don't insult me before I'm properly awake. It's not fair.' Papa yawned, wincing at the pain it caused him. He lay his forehead back upon the floorboards. 'And even if I did snore, it would be very rude of you to let me know. You should suffer in silence.'

'When can we leave for the ship?'

Papa checked his watch. 'We have a little time yet. We should have something to eat.'

Malik watched the cat sniff at the empty tin of food. 'I bet the cat won't like being on a ship.'

'You can't take it with you, Malik. They won't allow it.'

Malik's eyes widened. 'But I can't leave it. It hasn't got anyone to look after it.'

Papa got to his feet slowly. He folded his arms and waited for Malik to give in.

Malik folded his arms the same way. 'I won't leave without it.'

'But they won't let you on the ship with a cat. Think about Mama. She'll be on the ship. You wouldn't let her sail away on her own, would you?' Papa stretched backwards, one hand pressed against the bottom of his spine.

Malik could feel the panic rising in his chest. 'But Papa, I can't leave the cat here. It doesn't have any food and there won't be anyone to look after it. It *has* to come on the ship.'

'Oh, good grief.' Papa walked across to the window and looked down into the street. He held his beard as he thought about it. 'Of course, there is a well-known way. It's sailing close to the wind, but it might work.' Papa turned back to Malik with a glint in his eye. 'Surely I don't have to tell you how it's done? No?' Papa came and put an arm around Malik's shoulder. He almost whispered. 'You have to smuggle a cat on board a ship. That's the way it's always been done – it's a seafaring tradition. No one ever allows a cat on board a ship, but if you can smuggle it on, then once it's there and the ship has set sail – well, that's a different story.' Malik listened to Papa carefully. 'When the cat is finally discovered,

127

you must go and see the purser. He's the proper man to decide. On a ship the purser's word is law.'

'Not the captain?'

'The captain decides everything to do with the sailing of the ship, but it's the purser who makes it run smoothly. He will know that everyone loves a cat. It catches mice and keeps the men happy. So although it's officially forbidden, the purser will allow it. And anyway, what choice does he really have? I've never met a man who is so heartless that he would throw a cat overboard.'

Malik knew that Papa would find a way – Papa knew how things were done and Malik was happy with that.

Papa nodded toward the hall. 'Have they gone, do you think?'

'I don't know. I haven't heard them but I haven't been downstairs.'

'No, of course not. Just as I told you. That's right.' Papa had the rucksack on his knee. 'What do you want for breakfast?'

'Chocolate.'

'I might have known.' Papa took out the food that he had been given last night and spread it on the floor. He unwrapped the cheese, took the silver foil from the chocolate and broke away two segments. He handed them to Malik. 'Do you want cheese with that?'

Malik made a face. No one ate cheese and chocolate together.

Papa took his knife, cut a square of the hard yellow cheese, the same size as the chocolate, placed one on top of the other and popped it in his mouth. He chewed once, then held his hand up and spat it out. 'Oh, that hurt. I shouldn't have done that.' He put a hand to his jaw and held it gently.

'Didn't it taste good?' asked Malik.

'Hmmm? I'm not sure.' Papa licked his lips. 'It's not bad. If I could chew it properly it would be better. An acquired taste, I think. Something of a speciality.' He shook the lump of half-chewed food from his hand so it fell to the floor and he left it there.

There were footsteps in the room below them and the front door opened and closed. 'That'll be them downstairs,' said Papa. 'We should get ourselves ready.'

'What about the cat?' asked Malik.

Papa handed Malik the remaining chocolate and gave him a banana from the rucksack pocket, then he took out some of his own clothes and placed them on the floor next to him. He unfolded his knife and used the point to make a series of small holes in the side of the canvas.

Malik went over to the window as he ate the banana. 'There are people leaving the houses, Papa. They're going down to the dock.'

'We should hurry.' Papa nodded at the rucksack. 'See? I put some holes in the side for the cat to breathe. Waste of a good rucksack, but it should work. I warn you, though, the cat won't like it. It will whine for a while but it should settle down OK. Where is it? We should put it in now. Give it a chance to get used to it.'

Malik fetched the cat from the corner of the room. He held it under the front legs and Papa opened the top as wide as he could and Malik put the cat on top of the clothes and held it down as they pulled on the cord to close the edges over the animal.

The cat whined and cried, and it scratched at the side of the canvas. Malik wanted to open the bag up again and let it out. He fingered the holes in the canvas. 'It doesn't like it.'

'No. I don't expect it does. But it won't last for ever.'

Malik sucked at his bottom lip and frowned. 'If it's not quiet, we'll get caught.'

'It'll calm down once it's used to it.' Papa lifted up the sack and held it out. 'Here. Come and put this rucksack on. It's better that you carry it for the time being.'

Malik saw a small nose pressed against the holes as he put his arms through the straps. 'It'll be all right,' he whispered to the cat. 'You can trust me. Just wait till we're on the ship. Just wait till you meet Mama.'

The air was clear and fresh when Papa stepped onto the pavement, pulling Malik by the hand. Now that the cottages were occupied, the street had assumed a semblance of normality. There were curtains drawn across windows where none had been before, and a shirt had been washed out and hung up to dry from an upstairs sash – Malik thought he could even smell bacon. He wanted to stand still and breathe it in but Papa started toward the dock and Malik had to follow.

They walked at a quick pace. A horn sounded from the direction of the docks and a bird answered with a shrill call from the cottage roof above their heads. Everything was moving. A family stepped into their path from the front door of the cottage ahead of them – a mother, father and two girls of a similar age to Malik. The mother shouted up the stairs for the last of them to hurry up. 'Come on, Joey. It doesn't matter if the case won't lock.' Papa stepped from the kerb to give the family space and Malik looked into the house as they passed and saw a boy struggling down the stairs with a suitcase.

'Keep up,' said Papa briskly. Malik quickened his pace, which meant he had to run every few steps, and when he ran the rucksack bounced on his back and the cat gave a loud 'Meow' and scratched at the canvas behind Malik's head.

All this hurrying made Malik anxious and the butterflies returned to his stomach. Why did they need to hurry? Why did they need to arrive before everyone else? Ahead of them, a couple slammed a front door by pulling at the handle above the letterbox. What if there were too many people? What if Papa couldn't get tickets for the ship? What if Mama got delayed? Malik suddenly had a hundred questions in his head.

They walked on. A car came up the street behind them and Papa stepped back onto the pavement to let it past. Malik saw a family inside, with four of them on the back seat clutching bags.

Papa marched around the corner and on toward the chain-link fence. A jeep was parked at the entrance to the docks, just the same as there had been the previous day. This time there were three soldiers slouched in the leather seats. Malik got a better look at the charred cockpit of the stricken plane, but he knew not to ask if he could climb inside, and Papa held his hand so tightly that he couldn't pause for more than a moment and had to look back over his shoulder to get a proper look at it.

They strode onto the wide strip of concrete on the outskirts of the port. This was once where trucks would have parked while they waited to embark, but now the strip was full of armoured vehicles and trucks with canvas covers, painted green and black for camouflage. Malik saw a grey tank like the one that had paused outside the cottage, and behind it there were two more.

Ahead of Malik, the ship was huge. It had a navy blue hull that towered into the air, with three tiers of decks, set one on top of the other like a wedding cake, each with bright white rails that ran around their edge. A single blue funnel rose from the middle of the ship. They walked toward it.

When they were closer, Papa slowed to a stop and looked around him. 'Where did all these people come from?' he asked.

Malik saw that a metal railing had been erected along the quay in front of the ship. Armed soldiers were strung out along its length to prevent anyone reaching the front and rear gangplanks. A line of passengers pressed up against the rail and more passengers were loosely gathered on the dock behind them.

Papa tightened his hand around Malik's fingers. 'Stay close to me. Do you hear?'

Malik was worried about the cat on his back. He imagined it sitting in the little dark space, too terrified to even make a noise. He wanted to take the rucksack off and open it up, but Papa wasn't about to stop now. He was making his way through the crowd, stepping to the left and the right to avoid people that walked slower than they did. Malik was jerked quickly to one side as Papa pulled him out of the way of a truck which cut across their path sounding its horn, scattering the crowd.

Papa changed direction, making for the back of

the dock, toward the warehouse and Port Authority buildings where the crowd thinned out and people were able to move more easily in both directions. Papa stopped six metres short of the red doors and Malik looked eagerly to see whether Mama was waiting at the entrance, though he could see she wasn't there. Four men stood close to the warehouse entrance smoking twisted cigarettes they had rolled themselves, and on the far side of the doorway three women lay on hospital trolleys in the company of a cluster of nuns.

Malik said, 'I can't see Mama.'

'We're early,' Papa replied, and he leaned against the wall of the warehouse. 'There's plenty of time yet.'

Above them was a billboard with an advertisement for Imperial Stout. Malik stood back and looked up at it – it showed a smiling man with a long black beard, holding a glass of dark beer.

'But this is where we're meeting her?'

'Yes, this is the place.' Papa had to raise his voice against a convoy of trucks, which had driven onto the quayside and came to a stop at the foot of the crane. They carried crates stencilled with the words CENTRAL MUSEUM. 'I have to go and see my contact now but I want you here when I return.' Papa gave Malik one of his stern looks. 'Do you understand?'

'Can't I come with you?'

'No, Malik. Stay right here and don't move a muscle. You need to be here so that Mama can see you.'

Malik nodded. 'I'll stay right here, Papa.'

An official with a clipboard and megaphone hurried past them and turned into the crowd. Malik pointed at him and tugged Papa's sleeve. 'Is that the man you know?'

Papa glimpsed the man passing through a line of dockers wearing overalls and cloth caps. 'No, that's not him. He's just a ticket collector, isn't he? My man won't leave his desk. He'll be inside. I shouldn't be too long.'

Papa walked to the building's red door and went inside.

In the hall of the Port Authority building there were a lot more people than before. Soldiers stood at the red painted door when Papa reached the top of the staircase. 'I'm here for Nicholas Massa,' he told them.

A voice came from inside. 'Who are you?'

'Salvatore Bartholomew.' Papa stretched to see inside the crowded room. 'We spoke yesterday.' He heard Massa's voice, saw his face turn quickly to the door and Papa waved the papers that he had taken from his jacket.

'Let him in,' Massa ordered, and the soldiers moved either side of the door and Papa walked into a crowded office, thick with the smoke of cigars. The sun sent a stream of light through a tall window and onto a desk in the middle of the room. There were men in suits and others in shirt sleeves who wore guns hung from their shoulders on leather straps. Papa handed Massa the papers marked BARTHOLOMEW ENTERPRISE – IMPORT & EXPORT and Massa called his lawyers over to the table and two of them bent over and sifted through the papers.

Papa walked to the window and stood at the glass. He could see the crowd below him and the ship at the edge of the quay. During better times, he had stood at this window and watched ships arrive with the parts and raw materials for his factory. He had seen the same ships leave with the goods that he had manufactured and which he had sold around the world.

'How much of your business has been left intact?'
Massa shouted at his back.

Papa turned and answered him. 'The factory
should be safe, for sure. It may have been looted but
there has been no shelling in that area as far as I
know and most of the machinery is too large to steal
easily. But then it's my reputation that's important
for you. You won't be making anything, eh? People
don't ask questions when they see my name on the
side of a box.'

Massa walked over to Papa's shoulder.
'Nevertheless, it's always good to have something
solid to put your finger on. What of the warehouses?'

'The two largest, that are close to the factory,
should be intact, though we have lost the depot
down here by the port. I am sure of that.'

Massa looked at each of his men. 'Is everything
in order?'

The lawyers shrugged. They turned a page. 'He
just needs to sign.'

'Can I see the passenger list?' Papa looked
between the lawyers and Massa. 'I'd like to check
Malik's details are correct.'

Massa pointed to another desk in the corner of
the office. 'Those men will sort everything for you.'

'And what about my daughter?' Papa asked. 'Have you found her?'

Massa was already leaving the room. 'I told you, I don't make promises.'

The lawyer held the papers up ready to be signed. There was only so far you could push these men, and Papa knew that. He signed, then walked back to the window while they amended the ship's passenger list. To his left, Papa could see the edge of the Imperial Stout poster, and he followed the big bushy beard on it down towards the ground till he caught sight of Malik, standing directly below the glass of beer, waiting patiently.

Now that the port was safe, it might reopen to ships very soon. They would arrive from all over the world, bringing boxes with Papa's name stencilled on the side, the same as they had done for the past thirty years. They would be loaded into lorries by the big black crane and taken to the factory or to one of the warehouses that Papa owned, and where Nicholas Massa would now send men to recover whatever he planned to smuggle in the bottom of the boxes.

Ten metres along the wall from Malik, a man stood at his brazier roasting chestnuts on an upturned dustbin lid. Malik used him as a place to start, and then turned slowly, looking to the left and right as he checked the faces of everyone in the crowd.

There were so many to take in. Too many. It would be easy to miss a familiar face, even if they were near to him. The cat scratched at the side of the rucksack close to the back of Malik's head and he turned and caught sight of the clock on the Port Authority building. It said 9.45.

Malik looked past the family who had arrived next to him and were settling their children down, getting them to sit on their suitcases. The mother wiped the nose of the little girl and unbuttoned her yellow jacket to keep her from getting too hot now that the sun was up.

Papa was taking a long time. Malik thought about going into the warehouse to look for him, but then he might miss Mama if she arrived. No, he should stay where he was. He checked the Port Authority clock again and it had hardly moved. Perhaps it wasn't working.

Malik searched the crowd again. This time he tried to filter out all the faces of the men, so that he only saw the women. He stood on tiptoes and tried to put her face to the front of his head – he should see nothing else but her, and he should concentrate only on her face.

A clamour rose up from the entrance to the dock, where the armoured vehicles were parked. Malik saw two lines of soldiers marching onto the quayside and another line of soldiers had moved across the dock and were holding people back, their arms linked, their hands gripping the butts of their rifles.

The man with the clipboard hurried past Malik. He had the megaphone up at his mouth and was shouting for everyone with a ticket to form queues, so that they were ready when the time came to board. He pointed out different queues for the different coloured tickets – yellow to the right, and blue to the left.

Malik wanted Papa to come back. He stepped from one foot to the next. A thin line of smoke now rose from the blue funnel of the ship and the family beside him got their children to stand up and pick up their suitcases. The mother turned to the father. 'Where did he say the queue was for blue tickets?' They pushed forward into the crowd, so they were closer to the quayside.

'There you are.' Papa was suddenly beside him, his hand on Malik's shoulder, his eyes glittering. 'I have our tickets.'

'You do?'

'Of course. Look. Here is yours.' Papa held a ticket up to Malik's face. It was bright yellow and had the words 'the *Samaritan*' in bold black ink. Malik turned it over and saw his full name printed on the underside.

'Don't hold it up for everyone to see. Put it away, boy.' Papa looked the other way as Malik put the ticket in his pocket. 'Do you have it safely in the buttoned pocket?'

Malik nodded. He had known Papa would get them tickets for the ship. Now all he needed to do was find Mama. 'What's happening over at the gate?'

Papa looked back across to the entrance. 'They look like they're stopping people from coming onto the dock if they don't have tickets.'

'But what about Mama? Will she be able to get in?'

'Of course she'll get in,' said Papa. 'They have her name on the gate, but she's probably here already.' He looked around him. 'She may already be on the ship. It's not impossible.'

Malik felt the same pain as before. Mama was so close, but she still wasn't here with him. The sight of the soldiers on the gate made him stamp his foot. 'You said she was meeting us here!'

Papa bit his lip and watched the scene that was unfolding on the dockside. People had formed queues close to where you could board the gangplanks. Malik saw a man in a trilby push through a line and wave to his waiting wife and child to come and join him and the man with the megaphone announced that anyone with tickets should come forward now because they would board any minute.

The clock on the building suddenly said 10.20. 'Where is she, Papa? Why isn't Mama here?'

The two of them jumped at a single shot that rang out from somewhere on the dock, and the armoured cars started up their engines. Papa turned back to Malik. 'Your mother will be with the purser. I bet that's what's happened. She's probably already on the ship. Definitely. And you have your ticket with you. Perhaps you should join the queue while I wait here? You could go aboard and see if she's there, then you could wait with her till I arrive.'

'No, Papa.' Malik tightened the grip on Papa's hand. 'I don't want to get on the ship alone.'

Papa frowned. 'No, of course you don't. I was just thinking that would be easier.'

Malik shook his head. 'I'm not going on the ship without you.'

Papa hesitated. He tugged at his beard and held his hand up so that Malik would say no more. 'Very well,' he said at last. 'I will go and ask my contact if she has boarded. He has a list of all the passengers, so he will tell me for certain. But you should stay here and wait for me to come back. That way she won't miss us if she comes here as we had planned. Do you understand?'

Malik nodded. He looked around him, desperate for his mother's face. If only she would come. If only she would suddenly appear from nowhere, as though by magic, and put a hand on his head and smile at him. He looked left and then right, hoping to see her face, but it was Papa's face that appeared, suddenly close to Malik and large as the moon. He touched Malik's cheek. 'You're a good boy, Malik. I'm so proud of you. Remember that, won't you?'

Malik felt strange when Papa said that.

'Now, we must get on.' Papa took his hand from Malik's cheek and looked over at the bright red door. 'You wait right here.'

And Papa walked back inside the building.

The crowd was bigger than before and busier. Most of the people now faced the ship, so Malik could only see the backs of their heads. A metre or so ahead of him was a large black bollard and Malik climbed up to get a better view. To his left, the armoured cars were strung out in a line behind the soldiers, and beyond them Malik could see the people without tickets, still held back behind the gate, pushing against the line of soldiers. They were shouting and shaking their fists in the air.

Malik checked the women standing in the queue for the front gangplank. He noticed the colour and length of the hair that showed beneath their hats, but it was difficult to see clearly and he knew that he wasn't close enough to get a proper look. He put a hand up to shield his eyes from the sun.

Then suddenly he saw her, twenty metres away, standing alone near the back of a line, with blonde hair that touched the collar of her tweed coat.

Malik jumped down and ran in her direction, losing sight of her as he pushed past the backs of men who stood in the way. When he glimpsed her again she was still there. He wanted her to turn and look at him. He wanted her to smile when she saw him.

A lorry reversed through the crowd, its horn blaring, blocking Malik's path and forcing him to run around it, but when he came past its wide green bonnet there she was, standing right in front of him, and he took hold of her hand, but the woman, who was not Mama, drew her hand away and looked down at him, confused.

'I'm sorry,' stammered Malik. He wiped his hand on his shirt and let it fall to his side. 'I thought you were Mama.'

A man came past him shouting, 'Families to the left.' He sounded angry and waved his arms in front of him, trying to part the crowd. 'All those with children should be to the left.'

The woman asked, 'What is her name?'

'Maria Kusak,' Malik told her. 'She is wearing a blue dress with white flowers.'

The woman put a finger to her lips, concentrated for a moment and then dismissed him. 'I'm sorry,' she said. 'It could be anyone.'

Someone tapped Malik's shoulder and he turned to see a man whose hat touched the top of Malik's head as he leaned over him. 'Orphans should be over there.' He pointed out past Malik's head. 'There's a different queue for orphans over there.'

Malik looked across and saw a line of bewildered children holding yellow tickets just like the one in his pocket.

The man with the megaphone appeared and pointed at Malik. 'He's right. If you're an orphan you should be over there with the others.'

'I'm not an orphan.' Malik looked back at the Port Authority building, hoping to see Papa.

The official with the megaphone came right up close. 'So where are your parents? They should be with you. Are they here?' He took hold of Malik's shoulder. 'Can you give me your name? It's important that unaccompanied children are on the list if they're entitled to be on the ship.' He lifted his clipboard and turned the top page over. 'Do you understand me? I need to know if you have a ticket.'

A whistle shrieked above the noise of the crowd. Just behind Malik, a soldier was arguing with a passenger, telling him to leave the line because he didn't have a ticket. The man with the megaphone saw that people had begun to board, and he suddenly let go of Malik and hurried away in the direction of the front gangplank. The line of passengers pushed forward, then came to a stop. Someone shouted, 'There's no need to push if you've got a ticket. Please stop pushing. We'll all get on.'

Malik turned and ran, using the Imperial Stout poster to guide his way through the pressing crowd, till he stood beneath it and was exactly where Papa had left him.

Papa wasn't there. Neither was Mama.

He stared between the bodies of running men and women, trying to get a glimpse of either of them, his hands held together to stop them shaking. The ship was getting ready to leave and he was on his own. What if Mama was already on board like Papa had said? What if he had missed Papa as well? Perhaps Papa was looking for him now, searching the queues at the front of the quay? He should have done what Papa told him and stayed exactly where he was. He stared at the red door of the Port Authority building, deciding whether to go in.

A hand touched his shoulder. 'Are you Malik?'

Malik turned and saw a middle-aged lady in a black bonnet. She wore a white blouse that had large flat buttons done up to the neck and a jacket with a handkerchief in the top pocket. On her hands were soft black leather gloves.

A man stood close behind her. He was in a dress suit with a black bow tie. 'Well, are you?' he asked irritably, and he looked back to the line of passengers already walking up the front gangplank.

Malik looked from the man to the woman. 'Who are you? Where's Papa?'

The woman tried to smile. 'He asked us to take you onto the ship. He says you are to meet your mother in the purser's cabin and he'll be along shortly to find you both.'

Malik was confused. 'Papa told me to wait here. Have I missed him?'

The man tugged at his wife's jacket. 'Come on, Mariam. We'll miss our place. Come on.'

Malik didn't know what he should do. How did this woman know his name if it wasn't true? 'I want to wait for Papa,' he told her. 'He told me to wait for him here and not to move.'

The woman smiled sweetly. 'That's right. He told us you'd say that. He said to tell you that your mother is already on the ship and she's waiting for you. He checked the passenger list.' She held out her hand. 'We can take you on board. Your grandfather told us you have your ticket with you. You do have your ticket, don't you?'

Malik nodded, but he wasn't going to show her.

A roar came from the crowd near the entrance and there was gunfire.

'Mariam!' The man picked up his suitcase and slung a large leather satchel over his shoulder. He took hold of the woman's arm. 'Come on or we'll miss it. Let him stay if he won't come.'

The woman put her other hand out to Malik. 'She's waiting in the purser's cabin. Come with us and we can find her.'

Malik reached out and took the woman's hand. She followed her husband through the crowd and Malik went with her, walking two steps behind, the tip of her black leather glove in his fingers, turning his head from left to right to see if Papa would suddenly appear, but he could see nothing except the coats and hats of other passengers who were pressing to one side, penned in by the mob who had broken past the line of soldiers and were fighting to reach the ship.

The horn let out a loud blast and the smoke thickened in the air above the funnel. Mariam's husband waved his ticket in the air so the soldiers would let them through and they joined the line for the front gangplank.

'Tickets ready,' shouted the man with the megaphone from the foot of the gangplank.

They passed through the metal barrier and onto the empty quay, free of the crowd which surged and shouted from behind them. The woman asked Malik, 'Do you have your ticket ready?'

Malik looked back at the Port Authority building. 'When will Papa be here?'

'I don't know,' said the woman. She had creases in the skin around the edge her mouth. 'I'm sure he won't be long.' The dark blue hull towered up above them and the engines droned and throbbed. She held his hand tightly and they stepped toward the gangplank. 'My goodness,' she said in a breathless voice. 'What a big ship.'

When Malik looked behind him, the soldiers had closed the barrier and linked arms. Another shot was fired into the air.

'Tickets.' The collector put out his hand and Mariam's husband handed him two blue tickets that he took from the back of a calfskin wallet. The inspector checked them and handed them back. 'What about the boy?' he asked.

Malik unbuttoned his pocket, took out the folded yellow ticket and gave it to the man who opened it out and checked the number and the name. 'You're in the wrong line, but I can't see that it matters. The ticket's all in order.' He handed back the ticket and stood aside. Mariam's husband walked up the first steps of the gangplank and Mariam let go of Malik's hand to take hold of the white rail.

Malik took a step onto the gangplank and then another. He looked behind him at the crowd pressing around the barriers. There was surely no way Papa could get through now. He hesitated, wondering if he should turn back, but another man was already coming up behind him and he nudged Malik forward up the steps. 'Go on, son. Move it.'

Malik turned and walked up the stairs. He would go and see if Mama was with the purser. But he had to be quick.

He decided to run.

He ran past Mariam and on up the steps, pushing past her husband who cursed and dropped a bag. He ran till he had reached the end of the gangplank and stepped onto the deck of the ship, the great blue funnel rising up ahead of him. He ran along the edge of the white railings, past the cabin doors and the portholes, under the lifeboats hanging in their harnesses above the deck. He stopped and tugged at the sleeve of a passenger. 'Please, sir? Where's the purser's cabin?' The man shrugged and Malik took off again, his mind racing, trying to remember what his Papa had told him.

He found some stairs that took him down inside the ship. A sign on the wall showed the direction of the toilets and the first-class cabins. Malik ran down the stairs and came to another passenger deck, then ran down another flight of stairs to a deck that didn't have windows and he saw a sign which read 'Crew only', and he ran along the thin corridor, past doors that said 'Private', past a small kitchen where a woman was filling a teapot from a stainless steel urn.

A man came out into the corridor ahead of him and Malik shouted at him, 'I'm looking for the purser's cabin.'

The man pointed back the way he had come. 'Next floor up. Second corridor along.'

Malik turned back along the corridor and the ship's horn sounded loudly from somewhere above him.

The purser's door was closed. Malik knocked hard

and the door was opened by a man with a large black beard, who stared down at Malik. He looked very like the man in the Imperial Stout advert.

'I'm looking for my mother. Her name is Maria Kusak.'

The man looked blank. 'There's no one here. Who did you say again?'

Malik pushed past the man into the room, banging the rucksack against the frame of the door so that the cat whined. The purser followed Malik into the empty room, his head tilted slightly as he looked at the boy in the green Wellington boots, but Malik turned and ran back past him and out along the corridor. He ran up to the next deck, pushing past the passengers who were struggling with luggage on the stairs. A voice called out 'Malik,' and he turned to see Mariam waving from the other side of the landing, but he ignored her and ran on, up the next flight of stairs until he reached the door to the passenger deck, and he waited to let a man through before he put his shoulder down and barged against the legs of the next man coming in, forcing his way through and out into the open air, across the open deck at the stern, till he reached the back of the crowd that stood along the railings, waving at those who remained on the dock.

The deck of the ship trembled under Malik's feet and the red door of the warehouse was moving steadily to the right. Malik pushed forward till he reached the railings. On the quayside, the gang-planks had been withdrawn and Malik saw the strip of water between the dock and the hull of the ship widening. The horn sounded loudly and the crowd cheered. The engines laboured and groaned and the water churned and frothed against the concrete dock.

'No!' Malik shouted. 'I have to get off!' He barged his way back along the railings, past passengers who grumbled at him, dipping under the waving arms of those saying farewell to friends who had not got tickets, and the crowd on the dock shouted and held up their hands and some of them still fought with the soldiers.

The boat moved further away from the crowded dock. Malik heard a splash and saw a man in the water, who must have jumped or fallen. His hat bobbed beside him, calm as a duck, while he thrashed his arms and legs, struggling to keep himself afloat as his suitcase sank beneath him.

And then Malik saw Papa, on the very edge of the crowd, his hands in the pockets of his coat, watching the same man struggling in the water.

'Papa!' Malik shouted down to him. 'Papa!' He waved wildly. He was frantic. He climbed up onto the railings to make himself bigger and shouted again, 'Papa!'

The water below him was dark and deep, but Malik thought he could jump and swim to the quayside and he stepped higher up the railings until a hand gripped his collar and held on. 'Whoa there!' The man pulled Malik back down to the deck. 'Careful or you'll go over.'

Papa lifted his bruised and swollen face up to the ship.

Malik shouted again. He was sure Papa could hear him. He must have seen him. 'Papa!'

Malik thought he saw a smile, but then Papa turned and walked away from the edge of the quay, moving back into the crowd.

Malik struggled to free himself from the man behind him. 'Let me go! I need to get off the ship!'

The ship swung in a wide arc away from the quayside and Malik's view of the dock was replaced by open sea. He pushed his way back through the passengers, looking for a steward or a sailor who might be able to stop the ship leaving. But he could see no one. The ship gave one last cry of the horn as it left the port and Malik ran round to the railings on the far side, so he could still see the quayside. Was that Papa? Walking back along the edge of the dock in the direction of the cottages, his hands in his pockets and his head bowed? Malik knew that it was.

He turned and ran again, moving back along the ship towards the funnel, past the rows of wooden seating, towards the narrow stairs that would take him to the deck below.

He would demand to see the captain. He would make such a fuss that they would have no choice but to bring the ship back to the port.

And then he suddenly stopped, his eyes fixed on a family thirty metres ahead of him, climbing the stairs to the first-class cabins. He stepped to one side where a large metal winch would hide him, and then he looked again at the family who were already halfway up the staircase.

The mother guided her children with a hand on the shoulder of the youngest boy. She wore a large black hat with white feathers in one side and she had two sons, one older than Malik and one much younger. They were dressed in expensive clothes like her, with collars that were stiff and starched and hair that was washed and neatly parted. A valet in a crisp black uniform led the way with two bags of luggage in each hand, and at the rear of the party came the father, dressed as smartly as the rest, a thick fur collar on his winter coat.

And the father of the family was Angelo Vex.

Part 2

The purser's beard was thick and black and, being untrimmed, it made him look a proper sailor, with deep-set eyes that stared at the boy who stood before him in the blue short trousers and green Wellington boots.

Malik said, 'You have to take me back.'

'That's impossible,' said the purser. 'I have no intention of taking you back. Do you expect me to tell the captain he has to turn the ship around?'

Malik folded his arms across his chest. It was obvious that he did. 'My grandfather has been left behind. And Mama too.' He glared at the purser. 'I shouldn't be here on my own.'

The purser reached across the desk for the passenger list. 'Show me your ticket.'

Malik took the folded yellow ticket from the pocket of his shorts and handed it across. The purser turned it in his fingers and read the name that was printed on the back, then traced the column of type on his list, flicked the paper to the second page and traced again.

'Papa's surname is Bartholomew,' Malik helped him. 'It's not Kusak like Mama and me.'

'There's been no mistake. Neither your mother nor your grandfather have a place on the ship.

But you are listed – your name is on the register of orphans. See here?' He turned the list round and Malik saw his name added to the bottom of the list in black pen. 'Your ticket originates from the charity that has sponsored the allocation for orphans.'

'But I'm not an orphan!' Malik stamped his foot in disbelief. 'You're wrong. Papa told me he had a ticket.'

He *had* told him, hadn't he? Malik thought back to their conversation on the dock and tried to remember whether he had seen Papa's ticket. Could he remember the colour of it? The orphans all had yellow tickets, the same as Malik's, but Papa's would have been blue, the same as the tickets Mariam's husband had handed to the collector. But Malik couldn't remember seeing a blue ticket. He couldn't recall seeing Papa with a ticket at all. Only that would mean Papa had lied to him.

The purser tapped his fingers on the desk. He looked like he was struggling with thoughts of his own. 'How did you get on board the ship?'

'I showed the man my ticket at the steps. Papa sent a woman with a message for me to meet Mama in the purser's cabin. Listen, you are the purser, aren't you?'

The purser nodded.

'Then you must see that someone has made a mistake.'

'There's been no mistake, Malik.' The purser leaned forward in his chair. 'To be honest, if you're not an orphan, then you're very lucky to be on the ship – the allocation of tickets has been very strict.'

Malik clenched his hands into fists. 'I'm *not* lucky!' He raised his voice. 'I don't want to be here. I want to be back at the port.'

The purser sat back quickly. 'Please don't shout at me. It doesn't help.'

The floor beneath Malik's feet shuddered gently from the strain of the engines, and he knew that with each second that passed the ship took him further from his family. This was hopeless and Malik didn't know what he could do to change it. He began to cry. 'You can give my place to someone else,' he said quietly.

The purser reached for a box of tissues on his desk but found it empty. He shook his head, put a hand to his own top pocket and gave Malik a clean and folded handkerchief. Malik blew his nose. The purser looked serious. 'You should think about the possibility that your grandfather might have lied to you.'

Malik didn't want to hear this. He looked away.

The purser edged closer. 'Malik? Look at me.' Malik looked back into his eyes. 'Think about why he might have done that. If your grandfather couldn't afford a ticket, then the only way to get you on the ship would be as an orphan. Do you see?' The purser sat back in his chair. He took the yellow ticket from his desk and returned it to Malik. 'I don't know how he managed it, but he must have pulled some strings to get you this. He would have made some sacrifices.'

Malik stuffed the ticket into the pocket of his shorts. Papa had lied to him – that's what the purser was saying. Papa had tricked Malik onto the ship for his own good. Just the thought of it made him cry again and a tear fell from the end of his chin and landed on the rubber toe of his left boot. He lifted the handkerchief to his face and thought about all the things that Papa had told him in the last few days. Some of them had seemed true at the time and some hadn't. Malik didn't know what to believe any more.

But he knew one thing for certain. 'I'm not an orphan.' He sniffed. 'I'm not. You have to take me back.'

The purser folded his arms. 'I'm not taking anyone back. It's out of the question.'

Malik had one last card to play. 'There's something else,' he said. He took the rucksack from his shoulders and put it at the purser's feet. Then he opened the flap and stood back. The cat looked out from the top of the rucksack. 'Cats aren't allowed on ships.' Malik stood up straight with his arms across his chest. The two of them stared at one another, both with their arms folded. The cat stretched itself and jumped to the floor.

The purser leaned across the rucksack to take hold of Malik's shoulder. 'Listen carefully, Malik. A lady will be along in a moment. She is from the charity that paid for your ticket. When we get to shore they will look after you. They will make sure you're safe, with a family that will care for you as though you are a child of their own. It would be better for you if she thought you were an orphan, do you see? If they thought you weren't an orphan, it might cause problems. Do you understand?'

Malik shook his head. He didn't understand and he didn't want to. 'Will they send me back if I tell them?'

'No, Malik. I doubt they would do that, but it

would be complicated.' The purser let go of Malik's shoulder, took a deep breath and tried again. 'Your grandfather wants you to be safe. Isn't that what this has all been about?' He watched Malik's face closely. 'This voyage will only last three days, and when we arrive someone will take you to a new house to live with them. Once you're with them, you can think of ways to find your mother. Perhaps the family you go to live with can help you. You should think about that for the future, but for now, if I were you, I would keep quiet and be as grown-up as possible.' He tapped his nose in a way that Papa might have done. 'Keep quiet and keep the hope alive.' He clenched his fist and put it to his heart. 'In here, Malik. Do you see? You have to keep the hope alive.'

Malik was aware of his heart as a heavy weight inside his chest. But there *was* room for hope. If he had some hope, then maybe he could bear it. Only he would have to be patient. He would have to wait, and he didn't know if he could.

He remembered Papa's face lifted up to the ship as it had left the dock. Papa had spotted Malik on the rails and he had smiled to see him there, Malik was sure of it. If Papa was in his shoes now, he would work hard and plan and he would have reason to hope. Malik decided he would do the same. He put his hands in the pockets of his shorts and he had a sense of what it took to be grown-up.

There was a knock at the door. The purser hesitated, looked at Malik one last time, then called, 'Come in.'

A young woman entered. She had long fair hair tied as a ponytail. She wore a knee-length skirt and a thin beige cardigan over a clean white blouse. She reminded Malik of the teachers he'd had at school that were strict but fair.

The purser said. 'Miss Price, this is Malik Kusak. I think he's one of yours.'

Miss Price held her own list of passengers. She looked at Malik, found his name on her list and ticked it off. 'You were the one added at the last minute. Am I correct? I wondered where you'd got to.' She looked him up and down and she eventually smiled.

The cat came out from under the desk where it had been sniffing around. 'What about my cat?' asked Malik. 'I want to keep it with me.'

'It turns out Malik is a smuggler,' the purser told Miss Price. 'I think it's acceptable to have a cat on board for a few days. Would you agree? There's not much we can do about it till we arrive.'

So Papa had told the truth, Malik thought. No one was so heartless they threw a cat overboard.

The cat sniffed Miss Price around the ankles and she knelt down and tickled its neck.

'Can he keep it with him in the dormitory?' the purser asked her. 'Otherwise I will need to keep it locked away with me.'

Miss Price looked at Malik. 'You will have to take full responsibility for looking after it at all times. If it gets lost, there will be nothing I can do about it. Do you understand?' Malik nodded. 'And you have to feed it and clear up any mess.' Malik nodded. 'Well then, I think we can accommodate a cat. What's its name?'

Malik wiped his nose on the back of his hand. 'It doesn't have a name. I haven't found out what it is.'

'That won't do,' said the purser. 'Everyone needs a name on board a ship. If it were mine, I'd call it Booty, seeing as how it has white feet and was smuggled on board.'

Malik picked up the cat and whispered the name into its ear. 'Shall we call you Booty?' The cat licked his nose. It didn't seem to mind having a new name. Perhaps it – *he* – even liked it. Anyway, it was possible that it was his real name, because he did have white boots and there were only so many names you could give a cat.

Malik followed Miss Price quickly along the narrow, dim corridor, passing the cabins for the crew and rest rooms that smelled of smoke. They took a thin steep staircase up onto the busy public deck and Malik looked out across the railings. They were still in sight of land, though there were no signs of cars on the roads nor trains on the railway line which he could still just see, running past the derelict buildings that were scattered on the hillside.

Passengers were sitting on the benches looking tired, or they crowded the deck, standing in loose circles, which Miss Price parted with a hand on the shoulder and a curt, 'Excuse me.' She was talking to Malik as she walked. 'The other children are already settled in. Most of them are from an orphanage that was abandoned when the trouble began, but a few are new like you.' She touched his head lightly. 'I'm sure you will fit right in.'

When they reached the staircase where Malik had seen Angelo Vex, Miss Price pointed a finger in the air. 'The decks above us contain the first-class cabins and are out of bounds to you.' She passed below the polished shoes of passengers that stood at the railings of the deck above. Malik stayed close to the wall, so that he couldn't be seen if Angelo Vex were to step from one of the cabins.

Beyond the tall blue funnel, where the deck widened out to the full width of the ship, there were more rows of wooden benches where people sat holding luggage on their laps, their winter coats slung across their shoulders or spread over them as they dozed. A set of makeshift stairs led below deck into the rear hold. Miss Price led Malik down and he held the scaffold guardrail while his eyes adjusted to the low light.

The hold of the ship had been fitted out quickly for the voyage, using plywood walls that split the cavernous space into ten dormitories. It resembled the inside of a doll's house, lit by a cable of bright yellow bulbs that were fastened to the top of the plywood divides. Six of the compartments had been allocated to families and four were for the orphaned children.

Malik could smell sawdust and fresh paint, mingled with the sweat from unwashed bodies and the musk of clothes that had been slept in for too many nights. The sounds became different as he descended: babies cried like sirens in a blitz; the steel walls echoed with the scrapes of wooden beds being dragged into place across the makeshift floors; and someone would occasionally laugh too loud, interrupting the steady hum of conversation.

Miss Price brought Malik to a gap in the plywood wall, where a cardboard sign had been posted with the words DORMITORY 3/BOYS ONLY. They stepped inside. The room had four rows of bunk beds that wriggled with boys. She put a hand on Malik's shoulder. 'Find yourself a bed. If you see one without luggage or a child, then that can be yours.' She walked away, adding, 'I'll be back at six to collect everyone for supper.'

Malik looked across the dormitory hoping to see an empty bed, but he could see only limbs and faces and piles of bags. He thought most of the boys were the same age as himself, perhaps a few older, but then when he looked closer he saw boys as young as four, who stared wide-eyed at him as he stood at the door. He moved the rucksack up on his back, knowing that Booty was inside, his nose pressed to the holes in the canvas.

Malik knew he would feel more comfortable when he had found a bed. He took a step further into the room and then another, so that he could see down the aisle between two rows of bunks. There was a vacant lower bunk in the corner bed at the back of the room and Malik walked toward it. On the top bunk lay a long leather sports bag, but the bottom bunk was completely empty so Malik put his rucksack on the mattress there. He noticed that his bed had no pillow and that the one above had two, but he left them where they were and sat on the edge of the bunk, one hand on his rucksack, his fingers touching the holes where the cat put his nose. He was lucky to have a bed at all and he could use the rucksack for a pillow, the way Papa had done.

The other boys were quiet, either pretending to be asleep or reading books. In the opposite bunk lay a young boy in shorts, his knees drawn up into his chest and a comic held close to his face. Malik noticed it was only the younger children who wore shorts – all the older boys were in long trousers. He looked at his own bare legs and his green Wellington boots and remembered the long trousers in his rucksack.

He slipped off his boots and brought his legs inside the frame of the bed, then opened the top flap of his rucksack, took out the cat and held him close to his chest. The cat made him feel better and Malik stroked along his back till Booty purred and rubbed his nose against his arm. Malik felt a flicker of interest in the eyes of the other boys, and when he looked across the young boy opposite had put down his comic and was staring at Malik with wide eyes. Malik smiled, but he still didn't speak. He found his trousers and tugged them free of the sack. Putting Booty under his arm, he walked back along the row of beds and out into the corridor.

In the men's bathroom, a pipe ran the length of one wall with taps fitted at intervals of about sixty centimetres. Below it ran a stainless steel trough that was used as a sink, where men stood stripped to the waist with razors in their hands, their cheeks half covered in soap. Four men stood in the corner of the bathroom, changing into clean clothes that they had hung from the top of the partition. Their nakedness alarmed Malik, who was used to getting changed in private.

'Excuse me?' He stopped a man who was on his way out. 'Where are the toilets?'

The man waved a hand to the opposite wall where there was an identical trough without the taps.

'Those are the pissers,' he pointed out. 'Cubicles are at the far end. See? But I wouldn't go in there – you might never make it out again. Use the ones upstairs if you can get away with it.'

Malik could smell the toilets from where he stood, so he changed his trousers in the corner with the other men. If he stood facing the wall, he wouldn't have to look at any of them. When he was done, he walked back to the dormitory with his long trousers tucked into the top of his Wellington boots.

As he approached his bed, Malik saw an older boy bent over his bunk, sorting through the contents of Malik's rucksack, which were spread across the mattress. He was holding the roll of twine in his hand. 'What are you doing with my things?' Malik asked.

The boy ducked out from under the bunk and stood up straight. He was taller than Malik and his features had begun to sharpen into a man's. He didn't seem to mind being caught out. 'I was seeing what you have. You've got some useful stuff, but you shouldn't leave your things lying around like that or they'll get stolen.' He suddenly narrowed his eyes and thrust his head forward. 'Christ, you've got a cat. You'll be popular. Is he a ratter?' The boy gave back the ball of twine without even looking at Malik – he only had eyes for the cat. He stretched out a hand and tickled Booty's chin but Malik moved the cat away and put him down on the bed.

'You seem to have my pillow.' Malik took it back from the upper bunk and laid it on his mattress, then he began to put his things back in his rucksack – the screwdriver and pliers, the two candles still left in the box. Seeing them reminded Malik of Papa and a sudden choking feeling rose up in his throat. 'You shouldn't touch my things,' he told the boy.

'I was only seeing what you've got.' The boy sat down on Malik's mattress. 'Well, is he? Is he a ratter?'

Malik swallowed hard. 'I think so. I'm not sure.'

'It's worth finding out though, isn't it? It could be useful.' The boy looked around the room as though there should be a rat somewhere close.

Malik decided to impress him. 'I had to smuggle him on board.'

'Did you? So you're a smuggler? That could be useful too.' He looked over his shoulder at the door. 'Listen. You need to keep him secret. If they find him, they'll throw him overboard.' He paused. 'I've got cigarettes. Did I tell you?'

Malik shook his head. 'They won't throw him

overboard. No one ever does that to cats. Not if you smuggle them on board.'

'They will. That's what they do when they're not allowed.'

'The purser's already seen him. He says I can keep him. And Miss Price knows too.'

The boy looked puzzled. He stared at Malik as though he didn't understand what he had said, then suddenly he stood up, unzipped the leather bag on his own mattress and began rummaging about. Malik saw he was wearing a decent pair of long trousers and proper brown leather shoes that were scuffed at the toes. The boy ducked back under his bunk and held out a bright red cricket ball, so close to Malik's face that he could smell the leather. The ball was shiny and red like an apple, with crisp white stitches that ran in double lines around its centre. 'That's real, that is,' he said.

Malik read the words written in gold letters on the side of the ball: '*Four and three quarter ounces, hand-sewn.*'

The boy stood up straight again, reaching onto his bunk, and a moment later returned with a full-size cricket bat. He held it horizontally under Malik's nose. 'Feel the weight of that. Go on.'

Malik took hold of the bat and weighed it in his hands. He nodded.

The boy took it back and let it rest on his lap. 'I don't have a set of stumps. We could chalk them on the wall, though. Over there at the end of the room. We'd have to move those bunks to the side to play a decent game.' His hand divided the air in front of him and swept the bunks aside. 'You can feel how good the bat is. Proper English willow. It's a bit big for me but I'll grow into it. It's better that way than having a small one that won't last. Don't you agree?'

'Yes,' said Malik.

'Do you play cricket?'

'No,' said Malik. 'I mean yes.' He decided to come clean. 'Actually, I've never tried.'

The boy frowned. 'You've got to play cricket if you want to get on.' He took the bat away and Malik could hear him going through his bag again. 'I've got loads of stuff.' There was a clink of cutlery and a hand appeared, holding a thin wooden box. 'Dominoes,' declared the boy.

Malik ducked out of the bottom bunk and stood up. Poking from the boy's open bag was a gilt-edged picture frame and a silver candlestick – it looked like something you'd find in an antique shop. He held out a hand to the boy, the way he'd seen Papa do at parties. 'I'm Malik, by the way.'

The boy pushed the things back inside and zipped up the holdall. 'Oskar,' he said. They shook hands. 'I think I'll introduce you to Steffan. You'll like Steffan. He's got a deck of playing cards and a set of keys that can open every door.' He swung his heavy leather bag onto his shoulder. 'Come on, then. Let's get going.' He nodded at Malik's rucksack. 'I wouldn't leave that there.'

Malik followed Oskar up on deck. The sun had broken through the clouds and the fresh air felt good on his face. He looked for land but could now see nothing but waves.

The two of them walked around the edge of the deck. 'The thing about the next few days is it's all about money. It's about cash and making contacts.' Oskar swung his bag round to the other shoulder to prevent it hitting a man who stood looking out to sea. 'When we land we'll be in a strange place. We'll have no money and nowhere to live, so it'll be hard.

180

I expect they'll treat us like dogs. No, worse than dogs. They'll treat us like . . .' Oskar stumbled on his own idea. He wasn't able to think of anything they treated worse than dogs.

The rucksack was awkward on Malik's shoulder. He swung it higher. 'I don't think that can be right.' He held Booty with one arm and the cat's claws gripped his shirt and his ears were stiff and upright as he looked out to sea. 'The purser told me the charity who paid for our tickets would look after us. He was really nice to me, and so was Miss Price.'

Oskar shook his head. 'They may seem nice now, but once we get there they won't want to know – it'll be every man for himself. No different to how it was back home. We'll probably have to scavenge in bins.'

'Is that what you did?'

Oskar stopped walking. 'Maybe. Didn't you?' He watched Malik for a reaction, then stepped closer. He lowered his voice. 'I've taken stuff from the pockets of dead men.'

'What sort of stuff?'

'Anything. Wallets, guns. Don't you believe me?'

Malik didn't know what he believed. 'Is that what you've got in your bag?'

Oskar tightened his grip on the leather handle. 'I've got all sorts in here.'

Malik was sure he had. 'What about your parents? What happened to them?'

Oskar's face tightened and Malik couldn't tell whether he was about to cry or shout. He took a step back and saw Oskar's hands ball up into fists. 'You don't ask about that,' he snarled. 'You never ask anyone that kind of stuff. What's the matter with you?'

'Sorry,' Malik said quickly.

Oskar glared at him and Malik realized that, unlike him, these boys might actually have lost their families. They might have seen them killed. They might have lost all hope. He said it again like he meant it, 'I'm really sorry,' and he held out his hand.

Oskar hesitated, then accepted. 'That's all right. You're new here. You don't know how things work.'

Malik thought he knew some things. 'The purser said they would find us families to live with, not our proper families but people who would look after us as if they were proper. I don't know how I feel about that.'

The dark clouds had shifted from Oskar's face as quickly as they came. He answered matter-of-factly.

'I don't think that can be right. Why would anyone do that?'

Malik shrugged. 'That's what he said.'

Oskar shrugged back. 'I suppose you can believe who you like, but it doesn't seem very likely.'

His eyes flicked up and Malik was aware of someone standing behind him. He turned to see Mariam, the woman who had brought him on board the ship.

'I thought it was you,' she said to Malik. 'I'm glad I found you.' She fiddled with the clasp of her small black handbag, popped it open and found her purse. 'I have some money for you. Your grandfather asked me to give it to you but you rushed away before I had the chance.' She held out a fistful of notes that were folded neatly in half, the pink notes placed at the back.

Malik knew it must be Hector's money that Papa had tried to give him in the cottage and it made him feel uncomfortable. 'You keep it,' he told her. 'I don't want it.'

Oskar put his hand out. 'I'll take it for him. He's not thinking straight.'

Mariam looked at Oskar and dismissed him with a turn of the shoulder. She pressed the cash into

Malik's chest. 'Go on. Take it.' She took hold of his fingers and closed them round the notes. 'You should put it away quickly. You can never be too certain.'

Malik stuffed the handful of money into his trouser pocket and stared at the flustered woman. 'What did Papa say to you?' Malik wanted to know the truth of what had happened. 'Did you know him from before? Did he say what had happened to Mama?'

'Dear me . . . so many questions.' Mariam produced a compact mirror from her handbag and checked the powder on her nose.

Malik touched the hand that held the mirror, compelling the woman to look at him. 'I know I ask too many questions, but I need to know.'

Mariam nodded. She took a deep breath and spoke slowly. 'Your grandfather approached us on the dock while we were waiting to board the ship. He told us that he had got you a ticket but didn't have one for himself. He said you wouldn't get onto the boat without him and asked my husband and I to take you on board. He said to mention the purser, to tell you that your mother would be in the purser's office so that you'd come on board with us. It was all very last minute.'

'So you lied to me?'

Malik could see he'd caused offence. Mariam's features hardened. 'I don't make a habit of lying to children. Perhaps you aren't aware of what was happening in the town – I wouldn't want a child of my own left there. I expect you will understand when you are older.' Her voice softened when she said, 'Anyway, I wanted you to have the money. I didn't want to keep it.'

Malik said, 'When we arrive, I'm going to get a boat straight back and I'm going to look for them till I find them.'

Mariam nodded. 'Well, I hope you find them. I really do.' She lifted a finger to Booty's ear and tickled it. 'What a lovely cat,' she said before she left.

'Some people have all the luck,' said Oskar.

Malik took the money from his pocket, divided the notes and slapped half of them into Oskar's hand. 'Have this. So you stop complaining.'

Oskar pocketed the stash without hesitating, but he did say, 'I hope you find them too. I mean, if you ever go back.'

They found Steffan at the foot of the stairs leading up to the first-class cabins. He was a tall boy with cropped blond hair who held a large bunch of keys and a handkerchief in the same hand. When he saw Oskar, he hurried over. 'I don't think it's going to work. I've tried almost every key but they were getting suspicious. A woman said she was going to call the purser.' He blew his nose and the ring of keys rattled.

Oskar sucked at his lower lip. 'I thought you said those keys could open anything?'

Steffan frowned. 'They did before.'

Oskar was impatient. 'We'll have to leave it for another time. Come on, I know one more place it might work.' He led the two boys further along the gangway. 'This is Malik.' He glanced at the two of them over his shoulder. 'You'll like him. He's got a cat.'

Steffan nodded at Malik, then blew his nose again. 'Sinuses,' he said and sneezed loudly. 'That cat won't help.'

They stopped outside a steel door marked 'Out of Bounds' and Oskar looked around to make sure they wouldn't be seen, then he opened it and disappeared inside, quickly followed by Steffan.

Malik hesitated. He looked left and right, but then he stepped inside the door too and closed it shut behind him.

He found himself at the top of a wide wooden staircase that descended in two flights to a grand hall made from white marble. Oskar and Steffan were already at the foot of the stairs, looking up at a chandelier that hung at the full height of the hall. Malik walked on a red carpet that ran down the middle of the stairs – he couldn't believe what he was seeing.

'I found this place earlier,' said Oskar. 'This ship's a luxury cruiser that has been commissioned for the trip and they've locked this bit away to stop it getting trashed.'

There was a large set of double doors made from chrome and frosted glass. A shining brass plaque announced a ballroom. Steffan put his face to the glass. 'What's inside here? You can't see in.' He pulled at the locked doors.

'Use your keys,' said Oskar.

Steffan raised the large ring of keys and looked at the lock. He selected one of the larger keys, tried it, then removed it and selected another.

'Hurry up,' whispered Oskar, glancing back up the staircase.

Steffan tried two more of his keys without any luck. 'I don't think it's going to work.'

'You're worse than useless.' Oskar pushed him out of the way. 'Let me have a go.' He twisted the key slowly and listened as though it were a safe. 'No. It's no good.' He took out the key and thrust the ring back in Steffan's hand. 'It's not going to work.'

Steffan put the ring of keys into his pocket. 'That's what I said.'

Malik put an eye to the crack in the door. 'It's just a latch, a sort of lever.' He put his rucksack down, looked inside and found the screwdriver. He handed it to Steffan. 'This might work. Try and lever it up with that.'

Steffan slipped the shaft in the gap between the doors and lifted up the latch. He pushed the door open with a smile, and Oskar was inside before Malik could take a look. Malik followed Steffan in, shut the glass door and put the lock back in place.

The ballroom was the height of two decks, with full-length windows that looked out to sea along both sides. The parquet dance floor was polished to such a shine that it seemed be made of water rather than wood. Malik put Booty down at its edge but the cat sat with his face turned to the wall, refusing to be impressed, as though he came to places like this every day.

Above the dance floor was another chandelier, twice as large as the one on the staircase, with cascades of dripping glass that twinkled in the sunlight. Around the edge of the hall, pillars of red marble framed each window and large round tables were positioned at their side, each of them dressed with a starched white tablecloth that was sufficiently large to reach down to the floor.

'It's beautiful,' said Malik. The boys left their bags at the door and walked out into the middle of the ballroom.

'Watch this.' Oskar ran and dropped onto his knees in a long slide.

Malik turned full circle as he walked. He had images in his head of dancing couples twirling past him, and he thought of Papa's parties and Mama being asked to dance, but even Papa's parties were never anywhere as grand as this.

'What's in there?' Oskar pointed to a second set of double doors at the end of the ballroom, and they pushed them open and went inside.

The room was a casino, much smaller than the ballroom but with a lush red carpet and several smaller chandeliers. There were round tables with green baize tops, and each of them had a small wooden box in the centre.

Oskar lifted the lid of one to reveal two sets of playing cards and a set of five white dice. 'I'm having them.' He took the box from the table and went back into the ballroom in search of his holdall.

Steffan nodded toward the door. 'He's still in shock. At least, I think that's what it is – he only came to us the other day and I'm looking after him.'

'I thought he was looking after you.'

'We look after each other. He does things I'm not good at and vice versa.'

'I understand,' said Malik. 'You make a good team.'

Steffan seemed pleased with that.

'Where were you before the ship?'

Steffan didn't mind being asked. He said simply, 'At the orphanage. Most of us have lived there for a while.'

'Is that where the keys came from?'

Steffan blew his nose. 'I found them after the housekeeper left. They opened the pantry and the store cupboard there, and they opened Matron's office, only they don't seem to work on the ship.'

Oskar came back carrying his bag. He went straight to the roulette wheels over by the window. 'You do it like this.' He spun the wheel, tossed the white ball around the inside of the rim and they watched it spin and rattle on the pockets till it rested in red seven. 'You put your bets on the number you think it will be – you can choose more than one – and if it's right then you get twice as many back.' He took a look under the table and pulled up a tray with different coloured discs. 'Look! We can play properly. But we have to use real money.' He pulled the banknotes that Malik had given him from his pocket and put them on the table.

'Where did you get that?' asked Steffan.

Malik brought his own money out. 'Here, you have some as well.' He split the handful in two and gave one of them to Steffan.

Oskar slapped the sides of the wooden tray, making the plastic discs shake. 'I'll be the banker,' he announced. 'Winner takes all.'

They cashed their money in for discs. Steffan put a yellow on number six and two reds on number twenty-two. Malik watched him do it and then he put a yellow of his own on fifteen because it was the date of his birthday. Oskar spun the ball and it rolled fast around the outer edge and dropped into eleven. He raked in the plastic counters with a long stick. 'You can bet on red or black too,' he pointed out. Malik tried that on the next turn and he won. Oskar paid out twice the number of discs he had put down, flicking them over the table to Malik with his thumb.

They played on the roulette table for over an hour. Sometimes Malik or Steffan won and they danced around, shouting with their arms in the air, but more often they lost to the bank and by the end Oskar had all of the discs and the money lay in a single pile at his left hand.

'Are you going to keep it?' asked Steffan.

Oskar took hold of the notes and neatened the pile on the top of the table. 'I won it, didn't I? Fair and square.'

Malik shrugged. 'I don't mind.'

Steffan shrugged. 'I suppose it's up to you, Malik. It was your money.'

Oskar relented. He counted out three notes for them both. 'This is a down payment on your earnings.' He pocketed the rest of the money. 'From now on you work for me. And there'll be lots more where that came from – I've got plans for this journey.'

When they left the ballroom, the boys found the public deck had been divided up by makeshift washing lines, strung up by the dormitory passengers so they could dry damp clothes that had been scrubbed clean in the bathrooms below. Shirts and underpants hung like semaphore and two lines of dripping blankets divided the walkway from the benches, obscuring the view out to sea. The boys made their way between them, stepping over the legs of women who sat with folded arms and guarded their washing.

'Oskar! Steffan!' Miss Price appeared at the end of the line of blankets. She waved at them. 'I need to have a word.'

Malik turned to the boys and saw the back of Steffan's heel as he ducked under a pair of brown trousers and disappeared. Miss Price hurried up to Malik. 'Where are those boys? Did you see where they went?'

Malik was bewildered. 'They just disappeared.'

She pursed her lips. 'When you see them, tell them I want a word. There have been complaints from the first-class passengers regarding Steffan and a set of keys.' She looked at Booty, who was held in

Malik's arms. 'I found a collar for your cat.' She took an old blue velvet collar from her pocket and fastened it round the cat's neck so that the little brass ring hung below his chin. 'You will need some string if you are to tie him up.'

'I have some in my rucksack.'

Miss Price nodded. 'Very well.' She parted the washing with her hand and left in search of the boys.

It was then that Malik caught sight of Angelo Vex.

He was standing at the railings, some distance away, his face held up to the late-afternoon sun. He was smoking a cigar, or rather, he held a lit cigar between his fingers and smelled the thin line of smoke that drifted across his face and up into his nose. Malik caught his breath and jumped behind a red and blue blanket that hung close by.

What would he say if Vex saw him?

He should hurry away below deck before he was spotted. But Malik didn't move; some fascination made him want to stay and look, and he put his face round the blanket to check if he'd been seen. Vex had turned his back and was now looking out to sea. Malik recognized his wife in the deckchair to the left of him. She had her head back with her eyes closed, and her lips were red and glossy where she had applied fresh lipstick.

The deck was crowded. People walked past and others loitered, catching the last of the sun, so Malik thought it was probably possible to watch them and still be unobtrusive. He caught the eye of the woman who owned the blanket he was using to hide behind and realized she was watching him suspiciously. He tried a smile, then ducked between the washing and sauntered out a little way across the deck, still keeping his eye on Vex and his family.

He spotted Vex's older son, slouched in a deck-chair to the left of his mother. He wore a pair of slacks with a sharp crease down the front, a polo shirt and a woollen tank top. An open book rested across the top of his thigh and he was watching his younger brother as he ran past holding a model aeroplane in the air above his head. Malik knew it was a Mustang, with its tail fin and propeller painted post box red, as Mama had promised to buy Malik the same one to hang from his bedroom ceiling at home. He wondered if Vex had bought it using the money from the diamond. Perhaps he had. Perhaps everything this family owned – the smart clothes, the cigar, the first-class cabin – perhaps it had all come from the jewel in Papa's mouth.

Malik walked towards them. He no longer cared whether he could be seen. He hated Vex, hated all of them, the little boy included. He wanted to grab the plane and smash it underfoot, wanted to see their horrified faces as the child burst into tears. Malik took a step closer, staring at the back of Vex's head, and Vex suddenly turned round and looked out in his direction.

Malik turned and walked behind a white cotton shirt that hung on the line, his heart beating like an engine, but when he looked again, Vex had walked a few steps along the rail, completely unaware of him.

That made Malik even angrier. Was he so unimportant to Vex that he was invisible? Did he have to jump up and down with his arms in the air before Vex even noticed him?

A couple walked across his line of vision and Malik stepped out from behind the shirt. He watched Vex put the fat cigar to his lips, blow a light cloud of smoke up into the air and turn again toward the sea. Malik thought how when they had first met, Vex had told them he had sent his family away, so he'd been lying to them even before he had known about the diamond.

Malik should walk right up to him. He should point his finger at Vex and shout, 'Thief!' That would wipe the satisfied smile from his lips.

Malik did walk forward, but with each step he lost a little bit of anger and felt a bit more fear. There were fewer people between the two of them and the line of washing was a good two metres behind him. Vex's son ran past with the aeroplane in the air, making the sound of squealing engines and gunfire. 'Whoooaagh! Rat-a-tat-tat-tat!'

Malik couldn't even think what he would say if he got as far as Vex. He could point a finger and accuse him of theft. Yes, that much was easy. He could tell the whole world what he knew about Angelo Vex. He could even go to the purser and tell him what had happened.

But he had no proof. The diamond was gone. It had been sold or bartered and Papa wasn't here to back him up.

And now that he was closer, Vex seemed bigger than Malik remembered.

He would only just be able to point a finger in his face. And what would a man like Vex do if someone accused him of stealing? Papa had said he was one of the richest men in the city, and it would be his word against that of a child.

Malik took a step back and turned round toward the washing. Accusing Vex wouldn't get the diamond back. It wouldn't find Mama or get Papa on the ship. He was sure about that. Vex would probably just laugh at him. Yes, that was how it would be. Malik would be brushed aside and Vex would get away with it. He had already gotten away with it and there was nothing Malik could do except stay out of his way and hope that Vex didn't see him and cause trouble.

He shifted the rucksack on his shoulder and walked away. The boy ran past him and saw Booty in his arms, and Malik heard him shout, 'Cat!', but Malik didn't even glance back and when he reached the steps to the hold, no one had followed him.

He descended down into the gloom. A queue of women stood outside the bathroom, clutching dirty laundry to their chests. In the family rooms, parents had pulled their beds together and hung up shawls to screen themselves from the sight of others. Malik caught glimpses of them keeping their luggage and their children close.

He walked along the line of bunks in the dormitory till he reached his own bed. In the bunk opposite, the young boy with the comic was waiting for him. He smiled at Malik and held up a silver ball he'd made from paperclips. 'I did it for the cat.'

Malik put Booty down on the floor and the boy rolled the ball under the next bunk to his. Booty crouched and then sprang after it.

'He likes it,' said Malik. 'But he won't do it for long. He's not a dog.'

The boy offered Malik his hand. 'I'm Alex.'

They shook on it.

'My name's Malik and my cat is called Booty.'

Steffan and Oskar returned to the dormitory, bringing an apple with them.

'Where did you get to?' Oskar asked Malik, as he put his bag back on the top bunk.

'It was you who disappeared,' Malik objected. 'Miss Price was looking for you.'

'She found us.' Steffan sat down next to Malik. 'She confiscated my keys.'

'They didn't work anyway.' Oskar bent down

below the top bunk. He had a knife in his hand, and he offered Malik a slice of the apple. 'You should eat this. We won't get much else.' He nodded at the group of four boys kneeling with Booty on the floor. 'You could charge them for playing with that cat.'

Malik took the slice of apple and bit it. 'You're wrong, Oskar. We're getting supper at six. Miss Price will come down to fetch us.'

Oskar looked at Malik as though he pitied him. 'We saw the cooks making dinner. We'll be lucky if it's edible.'

'It's true,' said Steffan. 'They were boiling up bones in a pot. It smelled disgusting.'

Malik thought of the food he'd eaten in the past few days. Bits of bread and fruit and tuna from a tin. If supper was hot, it couldn't be that bad.

When Miss Price arrived, she made the boys line up in pairs. She put Oskar and Steffan at the front where she could keep an eye on them, and she made sure that Booty was left behind – Malik had cut a length of twine and he tied one end to Booty's collar and the other to a foot of the bunk, making sure it was long enough for the cat to walk a metre or so from the bed or to jump up and sleep on the mattress.

There were to be two meals each day, after the first-class passengers had finished breakfast and before the same guests went to supper, although today everyone was eating later because of the delay in boarding the ship.

Miss Price marched the children up the stairs and out onto the deck. At the door of the canteen they had to wait in line and shuffle in behind the boys from the other dormitory and the families who were already there. When they got inside the door, the room was stifling and smelled of stewed cabbage, but Malik didn't mind. He'd forgotten how hungry he was.

One of the dinner ladies served stew from a large stainless steel pot, a single spoonful per person. Another added two boiled potatoes and a forkful of greens. Malik could see the steam rise from the pots as he edged forward, could see the thick brown stew. He took a set of cutlery from the box at the front of the serving table and he held up his plate – he'd seen better food in his school canteen, but it smelled quite good once it was on his plate. He found a place at a table next to Oskar, who was already on his last spoonful.

'What's it like?' he asked Steffan.

'Rubbish,' said Oskar, with his mouth full. 'I told you it would be.'

Malik ate his supper. It wasn't as good as Mama used to make but it was still the first real meal he'd had in days. He finished everything on his plate and none of the boys had food left to scrape into the slops bucket as they were ushered out to make room for the first-class passengers.

Miss Price sent Malik to the kitchens for a plate of scraps for Booty. He knocked and asked for the cook, then waited outside the swing doors till they brought him a tin plate wrapped in silver foil and a small empty bowl for him to fill with water. He carried them back along the corridor and down into the dormitory, where he found Alex squatting on the floor with Booty on his knee.

'Do you want to feed him?' Malik folded back the foil to reveal some ends of cooked liver, chopped up small with a spoonful of gravy. Booty would like that. He gave the plate to Alex. 'Here. Put it in a corner where it's nice and quiet. Animals don't like to be disturbed while they're eating.'

Alex put the plate down just under the bed, then he went to fetch some water for the bowl.

Later, when Miss Price was sending them off to

the bathroom in groups of six, Alex came and took hold of Malik's hand. 'Can Booty sleep on my bed tonight?'

Malik panicked. 'No,' he said quickly, and he shook the other boy's hand free, then immediately regretted it. He touched the boy's shoulder. 'Look. He's in a new place with new people and he has to know that I'm here to look after him. Think how you'd feel if it was you.' Then he added, 'I'll put him on the outside of the mattress, so you can see him from your bed.'

Oskar shook his head as he climbed up onto his bunk with a toothbrush still in his mouth. 'All this fuss over an animal. It's just a cat, for heaven's sake.'

Malik tied Booty to the bunk bed again. When Miss Price put out the lights, there was only the glow of a single lamp by the door to see by, but some of the boys took out torches and read books or comics in their bunks. Malik lay on his back, listening to the hum of the engines that drove them on across the water. He had never been on a ship as big as this before. The wind had got up and the ship was rockier than it had been since leaving port. He imagined waves hitting the big steel hull and sending spray across the large white letters that spelled *Samaritan* on the stern.

What would Papa be doing now? Would he be back at the cottage, imagining Malik asleep on the ship? And what about Mama? Malik didn't want to think too hard where she might be, so he thought of her with Papa, the two of them together in the upstairs room of the cottage or, better still, back at home, back in her own bed, with Papa downstairs at the kitchen table, drinking coffee.

Booty settled himself down on the edge of the mattress, flicking his tail when Malik scratched at the scabs of old flea-bites which ran along his spine. His purr was louder than the hum of the engines as Malik tickled behind his ears, and the cat stretched out and arched his back. Malik put his nose into his fur and breathed deeply.

In one of the other dormitories, a mother began to sing a lullaby and her voice lifted up above the partition walls. Malik listened to her singing and he remembered the sound of Mama's voice from the times when she had sung to him. He could see her leaning over his bed, wearing her pretty blue dress with the white flowers on the hem, the same as she was wearing the last time he had seen her. She'd be wearing that same dress when he saw her next; he knew she would. Just thinking of Mama made him feel warmer and happier than he had been for a long time. He felt tired as he listened to the sweet, sad song and the boys around him put out their torches, one by one.

Once the singing had stopped, Malik heard a child crying quietly in the darkness. He looked across the aisle to the opposite bunk, thinking it must be Alex, but Alex was asleep, Malik was sure he was. And then he realized the crying came from the bunk above his head and it could be no one but Oskar.

When Malik woke up, Booty was gone. He knew it as soon as he opened his eyes. He felt behind his back with one hand, twisted round to double-check his bunk, then looked out across the other beds in the dormitory. The lights were on and there were boys on the move, some already dressed and some still in pyjamas.

Malik swung his legs to the floor. 'Where's my cat?' he called out, and he immediately spotted Alex on his hands and knees, reaching under a bed in the middle of the room. 'Alex?' Malik stood up.

The boy swung round, the paperclip ball in his hand. 'We were only playing.'

Booty stuck his head out from under the bed and sniffed the floor. Malik came across and picked him up. 'You can't just take him,' he said coldly.

'I didn't. He came to me.'

'Oh yeah? How did he untie himself?'

Alex had patches of red on his knees where the floor had scraped his skin. He shrugged. 'I don't know.'

Malik took the cat back to his bunk, where he noticed that Oskar's bed was already empty. Alex followed close behind him and picked up the empty tin plate from the floor under the bed. 'I could go and ask for food.'

Malik nodded. 'That would be good.' Then he added, 'Thank you.'

Malik took Booty to the bathroom and tied him to the leg of the trough as he washed and brushed his teeth. The men close to him scratched under the cat's chin and asked Malik questions about how old he was and how long he'd owned him.

When he returned to the dormitory, Alex was there with a fresh plate of food. He put it down in the corner and they stood at a distance watching Booty eat.

'What did you think had happened to him?' asked Alex.

'I don't know. Anything could have happened. I thought he'd disappeared.'

'There's nowhere for him to go,' Alex said. 'Anyway, he couldn't just disappear.'

Malik took a coin from his pocket. 'Watch this.' He flourished the coin in front of Alex's face, held it up between his thumb and forefinger then moved his other hand across it. When he opened the hand with the coin, it had disappeared.

Alex was open-mouthed.

'He's got it in his pants.' Steffan appeared from nowhere. 'I saw him do it. He had it in his other hand.'

'Thanks a lot,' said Malik, and he retrieved the coin from his underpants.

Steffan said, 'Come on, Oskar wants us up on deck now. He said we should have started work ages ago.'

The two of them went upstairs into the early morning sun. The sea was calm but Malik could taste salt in the air. They found Oskar crouching on the public deck with a stiff bristled brush and a duster.

He had written the word SHOESHINE on a piece of cardboard and propped it up on a footstool in front of him. 'You're late,' he said. 'I've been here for over an hour. If you want to work for me you need to be on time.'

Steffan looked across the empty deck. 'Have you had any takers?'

'I've had one, a fella from first-class.'

Malik turned over the coin in his pocket. 'What do you charge?'

'Ten.'

'Maybe it's too much.'

A man came up the stairs and walked out on deck. 'Shoeshine?' Oskar shouted at him, but he shook his head and walked the other way. Oskar stood up and stretched. 'It'll get busier. People will come up for breakfast soon. I've got a spare brush and another tin of polish. You should set up either end of the ship. I'll come and check on you in an hour.' He left them to get on with it.

Steffan blew his nose. 'Oskar's doing it all wrong.' He picked up the pen and altered the sign to read ORPHANAGE SHOESHINE. 'That'll get the sympathy vote,' he assured Malik. 'I've done this sort of thing before. People can't resist an orphan who's willing to work hard. If you sit on the floor with your cat, we'll get the pet-lovers too.'

Malik sat down on the deck.

Steffan took hold of the brush, put a foot up on the stool and began to clean the mud off his own shoes. 'No one uses a shoeshine when the vendor's got dirty feet.' He looked at Malik's wellingtons. 'Are they all you've got?' Malik nodded. 'Didn't you get something better at your orphanage?'

'I wasn't at an orphanage. I'm not an orphan. My mama is back in the town with my grandad.'

Steffan smiled. 'Sure. I understand.'

Malik felt uneasy. He put his hand out for the brush. 'I'll do your shoes.' He put polish on the tip of the brush and dabbed it on the scuffed shoe.

Steffan said, 'I went through the same thing.'

'Went through what?'

'Denial. It's a phase you go through. I've seen it with loads of the children who arrive at the orphanage. It helps to believe your parents aren't really dead. It's all about hope.'

Malik felt a surge of resentment. He wasn't going to listen to this. He said, 'Mama's not dead and I'm not making it up. As soon as we get off the ship, I'm coming back to look for her.'

'Of course you are.'

'I will!'

A man paused in front of them and looked down at his feet. He said, 'I'll get some money and come straight back.'

Steffan changed feet on the stool. 'Look, I don't mean to be a smart ass. It's just that I know how it works. Anyway, I think it's good to have a goal to aim for. And you'll need money because it's expensive to travel on a ship like this. Just don't leave it too long because you'll forget what they look like.'

Malik stopped cleaning Steffan's shoes. 'I don't believe that.'

Steffan nodded at the cloth. 'You need to buff them with that to make them shine. That's how it's done.' Then he added, 'Of course, you're older than I was. My parents died when I was six, so maybe it won't be the same for you.'

Malik picked up the cloth and polished Steffan's toes. 'Was it soldiers?'

'Course not. Not back then. It was a car crash – I was in the car with them, and I came straight to the orphanage from the hospital. I even missed the funeral. At first I knew they were dead because I felt so bad that it had to be the only possible reason but then, once the pain wore off, I began to think it was all a trick, you know, that they might still be alive. I thought they must have been kidnapped and held hostage. I spent a long time thinking everyone was lying to me. Then after about three years I forgot their faces. I just woke up one day and realized I couldn't remember how they looked, and that's when I had to admit that it must be true. I mean, if I couldn't even remember their faces, then they had to be dead, right? And they weren't coming back.'

Malik's mouth was dry. 'I won't ever forget,' he said quietly.

'It helps if you have a photo. Do you have a photo?'

Malik shook his head. There had been a small, framed picture of Mama by the side of his bed at home, but Papa hadn't thought to bring it when they had packed the rucksack with useful things for the journey.

Malik swallowed hard. 'What about Oskar? He wouldn't talk to me about his parents. Does he think they're still alive too?'

Steffan looked down at his shoes. 'They all do. That little kid Alex in the bunk next to yours, he thinks his mum is a secret agent who can't reveal her identity until she's completed her mission. Oskar's different because he's new. He's still in the painful stage. The soldiers shot his mum and dad in front of him, so if you think he's mad now, you should have seen him when they brought him to the orphanage. He'll still go through it, though. Everyone does. He'll start thinking they weren't really dead, that no one checked them and they crawled away to a doctor and got help. Something like that. But he's got to get through the pain first. He'll need me for that.'

Malik felt his heart as a heavy weight again, the same as he had in the purser's office. 'What if Miss Price puts you with different families? How will you help him then?'

'She won't.' Steffan pushed out his chin. 'She already knows it's both of us or nothing. If we can't stay together, we'll run away.'

The man came back and paid for a shine with loose change. Steffan took the money while Malik put the passenger's feet up on the stool and scrubbed till his arm ached.

After the first customer, there was a steady stream of takers as the deck got busier. Malik kept a lookout for Angelo Vex but he never saw him. He listened to snatches of conversation as he cleaned the shoes and he noticed a change from the day before – people were being friendly and telling each other where they were from or where they hoped to end up once they were off the ship. People were more relaxed than yesterday. Perhaps it was because they wore clean clothes. They certainly looked better than they had at the port, with the men freshly shaved and the women wearing lipstick or pieces of jewellery. They took photographs from their wallets and handed them around in the hope that they might find some connection to each other. Husbands introduced their wives and children to others, only to be told they'd already met that morning, in the queue for the canteen or using the bathroom.

'Where's Oskar got to?' asked Malik after they'd been working for over an hour.

Steffan handed out some change to a waiting man. 'I don't know. He'll be around.'

'And how much did he say he'd pay us?' joked Malik. 'I don't remember him saying.' They both laughed.

When Oskar did reappear, he had the purser with him and they carried a box of polished wooden discs and a set of sticks. They set them down on the deck. 'It's called shuffleboard,' said the purser. He pointed to a set of white lines on the opposite side of the deck. 'It's actually quite skilful. See those boxes over there? It's basically curling. Well, more like crown green bowls, really. You use the stick to push the disc into the boxes with the most points. You play it in teams.'

Oskar emptied the discs out at their feet.

'What about the shoeshine?' asked Steffan. 'We were just getting going.'

'Never mind with that,' Oskar told them. 'This is loads better.' He stood up on the railings and shouted, 'Clear the space, please, ladies and gentle-men. Shuffleboard match about to commence. Come and try your luck.'

The purser showed them how it was done, by sending a puck into the box marked with a ten, and then they each took a turn. Other passengers joined in, and once there was sufficient interest Oskar organized a competition, the *Samaritan Cup*, with teams of four people. Each team paid a fee to enter and Oskar announced a small cash prize, then drew up a schedule of matches to be played, allowing time for the competition to be completed before the ship arrived the day after next.

The purser told them there was also a table-tennis

table that could be put up in the viewing lounge and there was a game of quoits in the same room.

Oskar brought them all together. 'Right, I need referees for the matches to make sure there's fair play and to record results. We're also taking bets. Odds of up to four to one, but nothing more. If you're not sure we can cover the bets come and find me before you write out a slip.'

'I don't understand how it works,' said Malik.

'Right. You better stay here with me till you learn. Steffan, you take the other room. You all right with that?' Steffan nodded. 'Good. I'll be up to see how it's going in a while.'

Malik refereed the first game, which involved standing beside the boxes and shouting out the score of each new disc. He also had to keep a running total so that everyone knew which team was winning.

The passengers began to enjoy themselves and behave as if the voyage was a brief holiday. 'We may as well if we're here, mightn't we?' They cleared the deck of washing lines and stood in the sunshine, watching the games and applauding the winners.

The purser came round the deck and he saw Malik and put a hand to his shoulder. 'How's that cat?' he asked. 'Keeping out of trouble?'

'Yes, sir.' Malik tugged the string on his wrist to show that Booty was safely tied to him.

When the last of the first-class passengers had left the canteen, they went for their own late breakfast. Oskar stayed out on deck, saying he had to work through, but Malik went with Steffan and they sat by the window to eat. He saw the Vex children come down the stairs from the upper deck, and when he returned to Oskar Malik noticed the family name listed to play a game of shuffleboard that afternoon. His heart sank. He looked around to see if they were close, and although he couldn't see them it didn't make him feel any better. He never wanted to see that man again.

'I'm going back to the dorm,' he told Oskar.

'But you can't. You're my right-hand man.'

Malik shook his head. 'I quit. I'm sorry.'

'You won't get paid.'

'I don't mind,' Malik said. Then he added, 'I'll ask some of the other boys to come up and help.'

By mid-afternoon, Oskar had half the kids in the dormitory running the games for him and he came to find Malik. 'You have to come with me, I need you to do me a favour.'

'I don't want to work for you.'

'This isn't work. This is easy.' Oskar took hold of Malik's arm and pulled him up out of his bunk. He scooped up Booty and held him under his arm. 'I need one of your candles too. Don't worry, I'll pay you for it.'

'What do you want it for?' asked Malik.

'You'll see. Come on.'

Malik followed Oskar along the passage. They climbed the scaffold staircase and came up to the lower deck. Oskar walked fast, dodging past the legs of the passengers on the benches and avoiding a crowd that had gathered to watch a game of shuffle-board. He headed for the walkway that ran alongside a double row of six lifeboats, and stopped when he reached them. He loitered at the second boat.

'What are we doing here?' complained Malik.

Oskar smiled at a passenger walking past, then casually leaned his arm on the top edge of the boat and flicked his eyes to the orange canvas cover, and Malik saw a metre of cord hanging loose where it had been untied.

'When I lift up the canvas, you dive in.' Oskar

knocked three times on the side of the lifeboat. 'I'll hand Booty through and follow you in.' He took the loose edge of the cover in his fist and checked to make sure no one on the ship had taken an interest in them, then he lifted it high enough for Malik to fit through. 'Go on,' he ordered. 'Go.'

Malik grabbed the rim of the boat and jumped up, grappling with his legs till he was under the gap in the canvas and tumbling down into the darkness of the boat. He stopped almost immediately, the back of his head banging against the wood hard enough that it hurt. It was pitch-dark and the air was heavy with the smell of cigarette smoke. He tried to sit up as another leg touched his own and somebody sniggered with excitement. He heard Steffan whisper, 'Shhh . . .'

A box of light opened above his head. Malik looked up and there was Booty, a hand under his stomach, his feet kicking madly. Malik took hold of his cat and brought him down into the darkness. There was another snigger from inside the boat and Malik squinted, trying to see who was in there with him. He put a hand out behind him, felt an empty space and shuffled backwards on his bottom, then the box of light reappeared and Oskar suddenly came crashing down, his heel catching Malik's knee as he fell into the spot where Malik had sat only a moment before. Someone giggled again.

'Did you get the candle?' Malik didn't recognize the voice but he guessed it belonged to an older boy.

'Hang on,' said Oskar. He moved himself off Malik's leg.

There was the rattle of a matchbox, then the scratch and flare of a flame and Malik smelled phosphorus. He saw a pair of hands cupped around the wick, and when they withdrew he saw Oskar crouched less than a metre away, holding the candle in his fingers. Steffan sat hunched in the other end of the lifeboat, and either side of him were the sons of Angelo Vex, sitting in their expensive clothes, their legs folded, their hair parted crisply to one side and their black shoes shining in the candlelight.

The older boy held the crushed stub of a cigarette in his fingers as though it were still alight. Oskar nodded toward him. 'Malik, I'd like you to meet Marcos. You'll like him – he's rich.'

The older boy laughed at that. He nodded at Malik, but his younger brother didn't wait for an introduction.

'I'm Sonny.' The boy stretched out a green velvet arm, his fingers eager to take Malik's hand, and he shuffled across the bottom of the boat with his eyes stuck on Booty.

Oskar was in the way. He leaned back so that Sonny could get to Malik. 'He's seen you with the cat,' he explained. 'He's desperate to play with him, so I said he could meet you.'

Malik held Booty tight to his chest with both hands. 'He's mine!' he said loudly. 'He can't have him.'

Oskar put a finger to his lips. 'Keep it down,' he hissed. 'Someone will hear you.'

Sonny reached across Oskar with an outstretched arm, trying to touch Booty's head, but Malik shifted backward till his spine nudged the end of the boat. 'Don't do that,' he said. 'I don't like it.'

Oskar bent toward him. 'It's not a problem, Malik. Sonny is just like all the other little kids. He just wants to share.' Oskar put a hand on Malik's leg and smiled. 'He can't resist a cute cat.'

Malik panicked. He tried to stand but his head hit the canvas and he buckled over, tipping forward towards the boy till Oskar caught his shoulder and steadied him. 'Easy,' he said. 'Where you going?'

Malik found it hard to breathe. He pushed at the canvas above his head. 'How do you get out of here, Oskar? Let me out. I don't like it.' His feet were unsteady in the bottom of the boat and he fell against the side, grazing his shoulder on the wooden planks. When he tried to get up, he stumbled again and trod on Sonny's finger.

The boy screamed like a peacock.

'Hey!' cried Marcos. He lunged forward and took hold of his brother's arm, pulling Sonny out of the way and pushing Malik backwards into the end of the boat. 'Be careful!'

Malik gripped Booty tightly to his chest. He rose up on one knee and pushed a hand against the canvas. 'I'll shout for help if you don't let me out . . .' He saw the box of light appear and he pushed Booty past the canvas edge and let him dangle outside the boat before he dropped him. There was a howl from one of the boys as Malik kicked out with a foot, trying to get a hold on the edge of the rim, and then he was up and out into the air, dragging himself away from the canvas and dropping onto the deck in a pile, hurting his hip and elbow when he landed.

Malik blinked in the bright sun. He saw the shoes

of an elderly woman who had stopped to inspect him. 'Are you all right, dear?'

Booty was behind her, looking scared and indignant. Malik jumped to his feet. He said 'Excuse me,' then reached past her for his cat and walked away.

He heard Oskar jump out of the boat behind him – Malik didn't need to look back to know who it was. Oskar ran alongside Malik as he made for the stairs. 'What was that all about? He's just a kid. All he wanted was to hold the cat.'

Malik kept up his pace. 'I don't like them.'

'You don't even know them. I can't see the problem.' Oskar put a hand on Malik's shoulder. 'You let all the other kids play with Booty.'

'Not any more.' Malik held Booty tightly to his chest. 'He's my cat and they can't have him.'

Oskar cut across his path, forcing him to stop. 'If you won't come back, then let me borrow the cat. I can pay you for it. They've got money to burn, those two. You wouldn't believe it. It's just the little one – Sonny – he's crazy about animals. He had to leave behind a dog, two cats and a hutch full of guinea pigs and he's really missing them, so I sort of promised . . .'

'How much did he pay you?'

Oskar paused. 'I can cut you in. I would've, anyway.'

Malik pushed past him, but Oskar gripped the front of his shirt and wouldn't let him go. He swung him round by the shoulder. He was taller than Malik. Heavier too. He brought his face up close. 'I could take him. I could just take him and you couldn't stop me.'

Booty squirmed and tried to jump free of the two of them.

'Just you try.' Malik's lip curled upward in a snarl. 'You wouldn't dare.'

Oskar faltered. 'OK. You're right, I wouldn't.' He let go of Malik's shirt and Malik walked away from him towards the stairs.

Oskar followed two steps behind him saying, 'Listen, I'm just trying to understand. Because this doesn't make any sense. I'd give you half the money. No, wait a minute. That's not fair. *More* than half.'

Malik walked down the stairs to the dorm, past a group of running girls who wore blue school pinafores.

Oskar stood at the top. 'We could do a seventy–thirty split,' he shouted after him.

Malik found himself alone in the dormitory and he went through his rucksack, checking his possessions were all in order – it was the sort of thing Papa would have done. He laid out the screwdriver, the hammer and pliers and the roll of black gaffer tape with its end turned into a tab so you could find where it began. He opened out the blade from the handle of his pen- knife and slid it back again. Then he moved onto his spare clothes, unfolding them, shaking them out and folding them again.

The boys drifted back to their bunks. Oskar returned, full of spite, as he climbed up above Malik. 'You know they'll take that cat away from you, don't you?'

'I'm not listening.'

Oskar hung his head under the top bunk. 'They'll take him away from you as soon as we land. People don't want to adopt cats. He'll spoil your chances of getting a family. They'll put him in a sack and throw him in the water.'

Alex was lying on his bunk. He stood up and said for Oskar to 'leave him alone', and Malik had to say, 'It's all right, Alex, he doesn't mean it,' and Oskar said, 'Yes I do. You people need to wise up if you're going to survive this.'

Miss Price came down to take them to supper. She lined them up by the door with Oskar and Steffan at the front. Malik didn't want to leave Booty, so he stayed where he was in his bunk.

'Why aren't you lining up with the others?' Miss Price asked.

'I don't feel too well,' Malik lied.

Miss Price put her hand to his forehead. 'How do you mean?'

'I think I might be seasick. Really, I couldn't eat a thing even if I wanted to.'

Miss Price agreed. 'I shall come back with a bowl, but you must tell me if it gets any worse.'

After supper, Alex brought back a plate of fish ends for Booty. He took a bread roll from his pocket, which Malik ate when no one was watching.

That night, Malik attached Booty's piece of string to his finger, so he would wake up if anyone tried to take his cat, but in the morning when he woke, Booty was there on the edge of his bed, still asleep.

Oskar appeared to have forgotten their falling out. 'Are you going to help with the shuffleboard?'

he asked when everyone was up and dressed. 'It's the knockout stages this afternoon.'

Malik touched the large stainless steel bowl that Miss Price had given him to be sick in. 'I'm still not feeling too good,' he said. 'But thanks for asking.'

Miss Price looked at him suspiciously. 'You look better this morning. You really should try something to eat. Won't you come to the canteen?'

Malik shook his head. 'I really don't think I could.'

When the other boys left for breakfast, he untied Booty and let him roam about on the floor, then he borrowed one of Alex's comics and sat back on his bunk to read it. When he heard someone walk into the dorm and cough, he thought it was Alex, returning with a bowl of porridge that he'd sneaked from the canteen.

Malik looked up and saw Sonny Vex standing at the dormitory entrance, watching him from across the rows of bunk beds. His eyes were puffed and red from crying and he picked at the skin around the nail of his thumb.

Malik stood up and walked to the end of the row of bunk beds so he could see Sonny more clearly. He waited for him to speak, but Sonny just stood there and looked at him. Booty suddenly appeared from under a bunk, walking out into the space between them, and Malik ran and snatched him up. He raised his voice. 'Go away. I don't want you here. Do you hear me?'

Sonny locked his fingers together to make spires. He twisted his hands. 'Please . . .' he begged.

'No. You can't play with my cat. I don't want you to. Go and find something else to do.'

Sonny's face collapsed and he bowed his head. He wept silently, his chest rising and falling as he took in gulps of air, and Malik could see the tears that rolled from the small boy's face and landed on his polished shoes.

Well, so what? He was glad Sonny was upset. This boy had always been given everything he wanted but he wouldn't get to play with Booty. Not if Malik didn't want him to. Malik enjoyed seeing him cry.

But then he started to feel uneasy. He felt sorry for Sonny – he just couldn't help himself. 'Go away,' he told him quickly, to get it over with. 'You shouldn't be down here. It's private.'

Booty licked Malik's neck as though he were hurting and in need of comfort. And in a way he was. He was hurting for Sonny. He felt the hurt get bigger till it was the only thing inside him and then he couldn't remember why he was angry.

He reminded himself he was angry at Vex and what he did to Papa. But it wasn't fair to be angry with Sonny – he didn't even know about the diamond. Sonny had no idea who Papa was. He was just a little kid. Malik felt guilty, and knew he couldn't simply ignore him.

'Oskar says you like animals?' He said it out of nothing. He didn't want to start a conversation, it just popped out and even though he had a tone in his voice like he didn't care whether the boy answered him or not, he'd still said it.

Sonny nodded.

'He says you had a cat at home.'

The boy sniffed loudly. 'I had two cats.'

'And did they look like mine? Is that why you like Booty?'

'No.' The boy shook his head. 'They were prettier. Bits of brown and black and white, all mixed in. Your cat's not pretty.' Sonny became aware that he might have said something rude and he panicked. 'But I think he's a very brave cat to be smuggled onto a ship. Has he got a patch of white under his chin?

I can't remember.' He took a small step forward and stared at Booty.

Malik thought Sonny was funny – he was still at an age when he said something without thinking about the effect of his words, and though Malik didn't do that any more, he could remember how it felt.

'Come and see.' Malik led Sonny back to his bunk, but he wouldn't let him come too close. 'You stand there.' He pointed to a spot that was the length of a bunk bed from him, then held the cat up so Sonny could see the patch of white under his chin.

Sonny could barely contain himself. He so wanted to touch Booty that he couldn't stay still on his feet. 'I was right,' he said. 'He isn't pretty, but I bet he's clever, and even if he's not it doesn't matter. I still want to swap.'

'What do you mean you want to swap?' Malik stepped back. 'You can't swap anything. He's my cat.'

'I can pay you then.' Sonny looked at Booty with big wet eyes and he twisted the fingers of his hands together again.

Malik was almost speechless. Almost. But not quite. 'I don't want your money! I've got money of my own. You've got nothing that I want to swap. Do you understand?'

Sonny didn't seem to mind Malik shouting at him. He looked like he hadn't heard a thing that Malik had said as he took a step closer and put a shaking hand out to touch the cat. Malik shouted, 'Don't you touch him!' He made his voice quiet and threatening: 'He's mine. Do you understand?'

Sonny stopped, unnerved by Malik's tone. He put his hand down the front of his shorts and stepped from side to side. 'But . . .'

'No, Sonny. Now that's enough. I really do want you to go away and leave me alone. I expect your dad will buy you a new cat once the ship arrives. I expect he'll buy you a whole herd of cats.'

But Sonny didn't leave. He pursed his lips and appeared more determined than ever. He took a step closer, then another, and Malik stepped back till he had his back to the bunk and found he couldn't retreat any further. The boy was right there, only a few steps away, his eyes fixed on the cat.

'I've got treasure,' Sonny whispered. 'I've got real treasure, better than anything you've ever seen. Better than a cat.' He took a black leather box from the pocket of his shorts; it was the same size as a ring box. He held it in the palm of his hand and thrust it out toward Malik, and Malik reached out to lift the lid and see what was inside but Sonny drew his hand back and stepped away. 'You can't touch it,' he said quickly. 'Not unless I can touch the cat.'

'What have you got?' asked Malik quietly. 'Tell me what's inside the box.'

Sonny closed his fingers over the lid. He held it tightly to his chest, just as Malik was doing with the cat. 'It's special,' he said. 'It's a treasure tooth. Maybe from a shark or something, a shark who found a treasure chest and bit on a jewel so hard it got stuck in its tooth.'

Malik had to remember to breathe. He could hear his own heartbeat. He bent down on one knee so that his eyes were level with the boy and he put Booty down on the floor in front of him, holding him in place by the collar on his neck. He stretched his other hand out to the boy. 'Let me see.'

Sonny knelt down slowly, just as Malik had done, and he put a hand on Booty's head as he delivered the box into Malik's palm. Booty purred loudly as Malik let go of his collar and opened the lid of the box.

There was the diamond, lying on its side in the satin pillow, still attached to Papa's old yellow tooth, which had been broken from his jaw by Sonny's father.

Malik picked it up and the jewel sparkled in his fingers. It glistened, even though the light in the dormitory was dim. 'How did you get this?' he whispered.

Sonny was kneeling on the floor with both his hands in Booty's fur. He had pulled the cat close up against his bare thighs. 'I found it,' he said. 'It's mine. I can swap it if I want to.'

'You stole it, didn't you? You stole it from your father.'

'No I didn't,' said Sonny quickly. 'I found it and it's mine to swap.'

Malik took a deep breath. 'And do you want to swap? The treasure tooth for my cat?'

Sonny picked up Booty and cuddled him close to his face. He wiped his nose along his fur and then he nodded.

Malik's heart skipped a beat. He tried to think straight, but he couldn't while Sonny was there with his cat, so he looked away and his eye found an old sticker on a brown suitcase that lay on a nearby bed, half peeled and curling from the leather, showing fragments of a bright yellow sun and a deep blue sky.

The diamond for his cat.

Malik swallowed hard. He remembered what

Papa had said about the jewel and how it would make everything all right. That was what he'd said, that it would mean a new start for all of them, that it would make life easier. Perhaps it would mean he could afford a ticket for the boat once it was safe to come back.

Or perhaps Mama would come and find him before then. He imagined them meeting, maybe in front of a ship or at a new house. Malik would see his mother smile. He could see it very clearly, like she was real, right there in front of his eyes, his mother breaking into a big wide smile when he opened his fingers and she saw the diamond.

Malik thought he wanted to go to the toilet. His mouth was dry and he swallowed hard as he put the tooth back into the box and quickly shut the lid.

'If I do this there's no going back.'

Sonny didn't even look up from Booty's fur.

'Hey! Are you listening to me?'

Sonny glanced up and nodded.

'This would be for keeps.' Malik met his eye and held it. 'A deal's a deal. Fair and square. Isn't that right?'

Sonny said, 'Fair's fair,' but he wasn't really listening.

'And you don't tell your father. Do you understand? You don't tell a soul about this or I'll find you.
I'll find you and I'll take the cat back.'

Sonny breathed in deeply. He nodded again, his
eyes wide and eager. 'So can I keep him? Is that what
you mean? Is it a swap?'

Malik's fingers curled around the top of the box
so that it disappeared into the palm of his hand. He
quickly put it in the pocket of his trousers. 'Go on
then,' he said abruptly. 'Go away and take the cat
with you.' He sat down on his bunk and closed his
eyes, unable to look at Sonny and Booty any longer.
'Just go! Go quickly or I'll change my mind.'

Malik heard Sonny run four or five paces,
then come to a stop. He opened his eyes and saw
Sonny looking back to see if he really meant it,
and when Malik said nothing Sonny laughed out
loud and he squeezed Booty hard, a look of glee
across his face as he turned and ran from the room,
and the heels of his shoes tapped quickly on the
wooden boards till he reached the staircase and
was gone.

Malik's hands were shaking. He couldn't think, couldn't believe what he had just done. He wanted to run and find Sonny, but he couldn't move because in his head was the image of his mother's face, smiling at him as she opened the lid of the box and saw the diamond.

Malik put a finger on the box in his pocket, then took it away again.

He felt guilty even thinking about it. He was going to scream. Any moment now he would have to scream. If he didn't then his head might burst.

He ran fast up the wooden stairs and out across the open deck, unable to hold himself together any longer, running blindly across a shuffleboard court with tears on his face, kicking a disc with his foot so that a man shouted after him, but he was already gone, heading through the door that led to the wide wooden staircase and down to the ballroom. He slipped his screwdriver under the latch of the glass doors, flipped it up, then locked the door behind him.

He leaned against the frosted glass and his breath came in gulps and the tears wouldn't stop. He let the waves roll through him, great shudders that shook his ribs and made the air quiver in his throat.

What had he just done? It felt so big he couldn't fit it in his head. He had just made an orphan of his cat. He had given Booty away. And for what? For a diamond. Just a little sparkling stone that everyone believed would make them happy.

But the diamond didn't make Malik happy. His cat had made him happy. Booty had been with him when he was alone and scared. They had looked after each other until now. He must be heartless to have done a thing like that.

Malik took the box from his trouser pocket and opened the lid. The diamond glistened on its satin bed. It seemed to wink at him. He threw the box onto the dance floor and the diamond came loose and rattled across the polished wood, and he saw it come to a stop under the chandelier.

He wiped his nose on the back of his forearm and tried to take a deep breath. He needed to think this through. What would Papa have done? In the same situation, Papa would have done the same thing, Malik was sure. He would have done it for the same reason he had tricked Malik onto the ship. But Malik didn't want to be on the ship. So had Papa been wrong?

He stamped the sole of his Wellington boot on

the ballroom floor. This was too hard! And it wasn't fair because none of this was his fault. It wasn't. Not the war or the soldiers. Not the diamond or the tooth. Not Mama and Papa getting left behind.

And it was his diamond anyway! He should have just taken it from Sonny. No talk of a swap. He should have snatched it away. Stolen it back like Vex stole it in the first place. He could have done it easily.

Malik walked out across the ballroom till he stood under the chandelier. The tooth lay at his feet. He prodded it with his toe, and then he kicked it properly so that it skidded away across the ballroom floor.

He didn't even want it.

But he watched where it stopped.

He walked over to the tooth and picked it up. The stone was hard and cold. Booty had been warm when he slept next to him at night. Booty had purred for him. Malik turned the treasure tooth around in his fingers. There was still a speck of Papa's blood on the broken root that curved down from the gemstone.

Would Sonny look after Booty properly? Malik was certain he wouldn't. Sonny had even insulted him by saying that his own cats were prettier. No. Sonny would get bored of Booty soon enough. He would most likely get careless and lose him or let his father get rid of him.

The thought of Angelo Vex sent a shiver through Malik. He remembered him standing over Papa with the pliers in his hand.

Angelo Vex.

Vex was the rich man who always wins. Papa had said he was one of the most powerful men in town. How would Sonny explain the cat to him? He wouldn't be able to. Sonny would end up telling his father about the swap, even though Malik had warned him not to. He wouldn't have any choice. It didn't matter that Malik had sworn him to secrecy – Sonny was so young there was no way he could hold out, and then Vex would know everything and Vex would come looking for Malik.

Yes. He was sure of it.

Vex always got his way and he would again. He would come after Malik and he would get the diamond back and then Malik wouldn't even have that.

He closed his fingers over the tooth, then went and fetched the box and put the tooth back onto the satin pillow and closed the lid. The ship would land tomorrow, so Malik had time to think. He put his hand across the box and did a French Drop, moved it from one palm to the other in a single seamless movement. He may as well practise his trick while he thought of how to keep the stone safe from Vex.

Malik stayed in the ballroom till late afternoon. He would have stayed longer but he was worried about being missed and Oskar coming to look for him. When he left, he shut the frosted glass doors behind him and walked steadily up the red carpet of the staircase. He stepped out onto the deck and breathed the fresh air. A wind had got up and it sent salty sprays across the bows. He met the purser on the gangway and they nodded to one another. 'We'll be docking in the morning,' said the purser. 'We're still on schedule. Might even get there early.'

Malik had a sudden urge to tell him everything, but he didn't; he just smiled and walked on. The sun was already getting low in the sky as he passed below the first-class decks where the passengers dropped the ash from their cigarettes. He half expected Vex to come running down after him and grab his collar, but no one came.

The people up on deck had buttoned up their shirts and had jumpers or jackets to hand, in case they were needed. They had begun to look for land in sight. Families stood together at the railings and pointed toward the horizon, mistaking clouds for mountains and making plans for when the ship docked.

Oskar was on the stern deck, refereeing the final of the shuffleboard competition. He stood opposite the players, shouting back their points and keeping score. Malik went and stood by him. 'I decided you were right about my cat. They would have taken him away, and even if they didn't I couldn't have looked after him properly. So I gave him to Sonny. He'll have a better home with them than I could ever give him.'

Oskar was shocked. 'You shouldn't have done that. I was just angry. I don't know if it was true.' They watched a man slide a puck into the square in front of them and Oskar shouted, 'Nine!'

'Have you made much money on the betting?'

'I've done all right.' Oskar put his hands in his pockets. 'Did Sonny give you anything for the cat?'

Malik shook his head. He could feel the leather

jewel box pressed against his leg. 'I didn't want anything. It didn't seem right.'

Oskar said, 'There's something wrong with you.'

When the game was finished, Oskar announced the winner and held up the arm of the team captain in celebration and the crowd clapped them, then moved slowly away across the boat. Malik stayed out on the deck. He reckoned he was safer if he wasn't alone. He could see the first-class cabins from where he stood and expected a hand on his shoulder at any moment but it never came.

Malik went to supper with the rest of the boys. Miss Price said, 'I'm glad you're feeling better, Malik,' but she didn't notice the cat had gone. As they walked up the stairs in line, Alex tugged his sleeve and asked, 'Where's Booty?'

'I had to give him away. It was for his own good. I couldn't have kept him safe once we landed.'

Alex looked at him like he was a murderer.

Malik sat on his own in the canteen. He ate tomato soup with a fresh bread roll and a thick slice of breaded ham that had a rim of bright white fat. When someone passed the windows of the canteen, Malik would glance up, expecting it to be Angelo Vex, but it never was. As a special treat on their last night, there was sponge pudding with custard. Malik made it last while he watched the window and tried to guess what might be going on inside the Vex family cabin.

Sonny must have returned there by now and his parents would have seen Booty. Perhaps Sonny had actually thought up a story that didn't arouse suspicion? His older brother Marcos could have helped him. But did that mean that Marcos knew about the diamond? Marcos was old enough to know that the swap wasn't fair, and he would surely have told his father if he knew. Perhaps Sonny had hidden Booty? Perhaps Vex wouldn't discover the diamond was gone till they were well away from the ship?

Perhaps . . . perhaps he'd get away with it after all.

Malik finished everything on his plate then stacked the dirty dishes at the table where they collected the washing up. No. It was still too early to believe he'd got away with it. He should assume that Vex already knew. But what would he do? How would Vex tackle it?

He might go to the purser. If he did, they would come to find Malik and make him turn out his pockets in the purser's office, just like they would have done at school. Or Vex might come and find him on his own, rushing straight down to the dormitory as soon as he discovered the diamond was gone and Malik was on board the ship.

Yes. That's how he'd do it. That would be Vex's style.

Malik went outside on deck. He should be safe while the first-class passengers ate their food. He hung about, watching people play quoits while the sun sank lower in the autumn sky. When the strings of white bulbs lit up along each tier of the ship, Malik went below deck. In the dormitory, the boys were getting ready for bed. Malik washed and cleaned his teeth at the makeshift trough and then lay in his bunk, with his trousers still on and the diamond in his pocket.

Still no one came for him. He began to believe that Vex couldn't know the diamond was missing. He only had to sleep and have breakfast and that would leave just enough time to pack his things before the ship docked. Malik felt warm inside. He thought how proud Papa would be that he had got the diamond back and how all of the pain at the docks might have been worthwhile after all.

And then Malik realized that it wasn't over, that

he wasn't safe until the morning, because Vex would try to steal the diamond back in the night. Just like he had before. Yes, of course, that's what he would do. That must be what Vex was waiting for. Malik thought it through. Perhaps Vex wouldn't do it himself. He might think it was too risky. But he could pay one of the boys to do it. There were orphans here who would do anything for money.

Oskar moved in the bed above him. It seemed so obvious.

The lights went out in the dormitory and the boys who owned torches turned them on so that they could read. Malik decided he would have to stay awake. If he could stay awake all night, then nobody could steal the diamond from his pocket. But could he do it? He had tried to stay up all night once, when his mother had a party at the house. He hadn't managed it then and he might not manage it now.

When the woman in the other dormitory began to sing her lullabies, Malik put his hands across his ears and waited for her singing to stop – he had no intention of letting her rock him to sleep. He sat up and lifted his rucksack from the floor at the bottom of his bed, found his torch and turned it on. He checked that Oskar wasn't watching what he was doing, then he took Booty's string, tied one end round the jewel box and the other around his finger. He put the box back in his pocket. Now, if he did fall asleep, no one could take the box without waking him up.

Malik settled back down on his bunk. All around him was the glow of torch bulbs, like fireflies in the darkness. One by one, he watched them disappear. He lay in the shadow of the bunk bed and made his eyes as big as possible.

He missed his cat . . . This was the time when Booty would curl up on the bed and hold his head back to have his chin tickled. Malik didn't want to think of him but he couldn't help himself and anyway, the sadness made him angry and it was hard to sleep when you were angry.

He pulled the blanket up around his legs and tried to think of something else. He remembered what Papa had told him about the country where they would dock tomorrow. He pictured the roads with wooden houses and the white picket fences. He imagined opening one of those post boxes on poles to discover the letter that told him Mama was coming for him. He would be so excited he wouldn't go out until she came, just in case he missed her. He would watch the road till she arrived, waiting for days if that's what it took, till one day he'd see a woman in a pretty blue dress, carrying a suitcase, and she would open the gate and start down the path and he would know her then, for sure. He'd know it was his mama.

Malik's eyelids were heavy. He wished he hadn't eaten so much at supper. The sponge pudding was weighing him down, making everything heavy and tugging at his eyelids. He struggled up onto an elbow and forced his eyebrows back up his forehead. The breath of all the sleeping boys became hypnotic and he listened out for Oskar – Malik was sure that he could hear his heavy breath. Perhaps he had been wrong about him. Perhaps it wouldn't be Oskar who tried to steal the diamond, after all.

Malik didn't know what time it was but it was late. He turned over and the box in his pocket pushed into his hip and hurt, so he turned back again. This was no good. He kicked the blanket off his legs and put his feet to the floor, then stood up and stretched his arms above his head, only for the jewel box to pop out of his pocket and hang down his arm, right below Oskar's sleeping face. Malik untied the string from his finger and put the box back into his pocket. The whole dormitory was asleep apart from him.

He decided to go for a walk on deck. That would keep him awake. He slipped his feet into his Wellington boots and pulled the brown jumper over his head, then made his way along the row of beds till he reached the dormitory door. He slipped out into the corridor, passed the bathroom, came to the stairs and climbed up into the fresh air.

The night was cooler out on deck. The sea was calm, and moved in gentle ridges that reflected the lights from the passenger decks. Malik rested against a capstan and looked out into the darkness as the ship ploughed onward. The sky above was clear and full of stars with a crescent moon above the captain's bridge, and beside the moon were two green lights that shone at the top of the flagpole which flew the ensign.

Malik leaned over the railings and saw a line of white wash that led back into the darkness. He sat down with his back to the capstan and looked out into the night. Eventually the sky began to turn pale and the stars became less bright.

He had seen the sun rise once before from a window at home. He had been ill and unable to sleep and had lain in his mother's arms while she said, 'Wait for it, here it comes, here it comes.' And then, there it was. A great ball of fire that rose into the sky.

Malik hugged himself to keep warm. The ship moved easily through the water toward a thin line of red on the horizon that spread itself outward and upwards till the sun rose out of the sea as a perfect golden globe.

Malik smiled at the new day. He had stayed awake and the diamond was safe in his pocket. In only a few hours, they would reach the port and then he would have done it. The diamond would be his and he could begin to make everything in his life all right again.

A seagull cried out as it flew alongside the ship and Malik turned to see the bird but instead saw the figure on the upper deck who watched him with a look of interest.

Angelo Vex had a cigarette in his hand and a puzzled expression that suddenly changed to one of recognition. Malik's heart stopped beating. He put his head down and walked quickly toward the staircase that led to the dormitories, all the time expecting Vex to break into a run, to shout out and come after him. When he reached the stairs, Malik turned and looked back. Vex stood in the same spot, calmly observing him, still smoking his cigarette.

Malik hid in the toilets. He sat on the stinking metal bowl in the last of the four cubicles and his mind was racing. He told himself he must stay calm and try to keep his head. He must think it through.

It was bad that Vex had seen him.

It had been a mistake to go out on deck. A stupid mistake. But never mind, he couldn't help that now. He ran the encounter over in his mind, remembering the look of surprise when Vex had recognized him. So he obviously hadn't known that Malik was on board. Did that mean he also didn't know the diamond was missing? Malik couldn't be sure either way.

He tried to calm himself down. It was no good second-guessing.

He listened at the door but could hear no one in the bathroom. He should go back to the dormitory. He would be safer there. He slid back the lock on the door and walked carefully across the empty bathroom into the wooden corridor, then slipped back into the dorm.

He should behave as he would on any other day. He got back into bed and waited for the first signs of life and then, when the other boys were stretching in their bunks or hunched over putting on socks, he went back to the bathroom to wash.

Miss Price arrived. She told them breakfast would be early and they were free to take themselves to the canteen when they were ready.

Oskar and Steffan were discussing what a family would look for in an orphan. Malik followed them out of the dormitory and up on deck.

'They like them to be young.' Steffan sounded like he knew what he was talking about. He put a finger to one of his nostrils and snorted. 'The older you are the worse chance you have. That's how it was with the people that came to the orphanage.'

'We need shorts,' said Oskar. 'We'll get the little kids to give us their shorts.'

Malik saw a group of excited passengers gathered on the starboard bow, pointing to a strip of land that had been lit by the morning sun. Malik paused and looked across. He could see factories with smoke coming from big chimneys, and there was a busy road with sunshine glinting on the windscreens of the tiny moving cars. He was excited to get a glimpse of the new country and he looked back for Oskar and Steffan but they had already gone to the canteen.

He went across to the railings and stood on a bench so he could look over the heads of other passengers at the blue-grey outline. They had almost arrived. He jumped down and went to the opposite bow, intending to pass along the empty gangway and see whether any land could be seen from this other side of the ship.

A hand pinched his ear so that it hurt. Malik twisted round and there was Angelo Vex, standing close behind him.

Vex let go of Malik's ear and took hold of his shoulder instead, his long dark nail scratching Malik's skin beneath his shirt. He guided Malik over to the railings so that the two of them were alone. 'Why don't we move out of the way? I have something of yours to return.'

Malik saw that Vex carried a pink hat box under his arm. It had a large red bow on the lid. Vex took his hand from Malik's shoulder and removed the top – and Booty lifted his head above the rim and sniffed the air.

Vex smiled wide enough to show the gap in his front teeth. 'My son has a weakness for fur.' He offered the hat box to Malik, pushing it against his chest, but Malik refused to take hold of it, taking a step away instead. Vex raised his eyebrows and Malik knew he shouldn't try to run. Vex brought the box back underneath his arm. 'Never mind. But I believe you have something of mine?'

Malik was frightened. Up close, Vex was so much bigger than him. But Malik was also angry and he couldn't help shouting out, 'It isn't yours! It never was!' He pointed a finger. 'You stole it from Papa!'

Vex blew through his nose like a bull and his eyes flicked from left to right. 'How old are you, Malik?' he said quietly. 'It is Malik, isn't it?'

Malik stuck out his chin, the way Oskar did when he was annoyed. He wasn't going to answer.

Vex's eyes hardened. He shifted the weight on his feet. 'Well, it's of no matter. You're young enough for me to forgive your rudeness just this once.' A woman walked past with her daughter and Vex smiled and paused to let them pass. 'You should know that I didn't steal that diamond,' he said quietly.

Malik's jaw dropped open but Vex held a single finger in the air to indicate that he shouldn't interrupt.

'It's true.' Vex was calm and confident. 'I imagine

you don't think very highly of me, but nevertheless I want you to know that I'm not a bad man. Really, Malik, I'm not. These are desperate times and I hear so many stories. It seems that everyone has lost something. Some people have lost everything. But I didn't steal your papa's tooth. He gave it to me in exchange for securing you a place on this ship.' He lifted his eyebrows, daring Malik not to believe him. 'Why else do you think you are here? You couldn't afford a ticket otherwise. I'm surprised he didn't tell you, but perhaps he was embarrassed.' He tilted his head towards Malik as though they were conspirators and lowered his voice. 'Diamonds can be troublesome things. They're never easy to deal in – everyone knows they're valuable but they don't know how to trade them. Do you understand me? One can't simply go into a shop and give a diamond to the boy behind the counter. You need to know the right people. You need to have contacts.'

Booty mewled at Malik. He tried to climb from the open box and Vex brushed him back inside with his free hand so that the cat cowered with only his eyes above the rim.

'Your grandfather was out of his depth, Malik. He realized that in his own hands the jewel was as good as worthless. So I offered to help him. For a price.'

Malik shook his head. 'You stole it from his jacket in the middle of the night,' he said quietly.

'No, Malik.' Vex laughed softly and wagged a finger over Malik's head. 'You shouldn't make accusations like that. I met your grandfather at the docks and he gave me the jewel to ensure your safe passage on the ship. What's more, he gave me his blessing. That's the truth of it. You should be grateful to me and return what's mine.'

Malik suddenly felt like he would burst. He planted his feet firmly on the deck and raised his voice. 'You told Papa you had nothing left when all the time you had enough money to buy your own tickets. You didn't even have to sell the diamond. All that stuff you said about how your clothes were old. You were lying from the start and you're lying now. I know you are.'

Vex pinched his lips together. His eyes flicked from left to right, checking that the gangway was clear. 'Who do you think people will believe?' he hissed at Malik. 'Me or you, eh? They will think you're making up stories about me. They will think you're a liar. They will ask how a child such as you came to be in the possession of such a magnificent jewel.'

'I swapped it!' Malik shouted. 'Fair and square. A deal's a deal and anyway –'

Vex pointed a finger at Malik's face. 'I will tell them that you stole it from me. They will believe you are the thief, Malik. And they will punish you. I will insist on it. Do you understand me? They will lock you away and they won't let you out for a very long time.' He put the lid back on the pink hat box and thrust it once more against Malik's chest. 'Now take back your cat.'

Malik stepped away again.

Vex took a deep breath and ran his hand across the bald patch in the centre of his head. He drummed his fingers on the railing. 'I really don't have time for this. This is your last chance before I ask the purser to call ahead and have the police meet us at the dock. You should take your cat while you have the chance and you must tell me where you've hidden the jewel.'

Malik moved his hand to his trouser pocket and Vex saw him do it. He smiled widely.

'Unless you haven't hidden it at all?'

Malik brought out the black leather box and he

opened the lid. There was the tooth with the diamond. Vex's eyes widened and his tongue wet the edge of his lips.

Malik took four quick steps backwards and made a sudden movement with his left hand up to the box and Vex saw his chance. He lurched at Malik, but then stopped dead. Malik held the black box out over the side of the ship. His fingers were loose across the closed lid. 'I'll drop it if you come any closer.'

Vex's top lip twitched. He suddenly pulled Booty from the hat box, held him by his collar and thrust him out across the railing so that he hung like a kitten in its mother's mouth, all four of his legs stretched long and rigid over the open sea. 'Now don't be a stupid little boy,' spat Vex. 'Just give me the diamond.'

Malik dropped the box.

They both watched it tumble through the air, arcing left then right before it hit the dark water and sank from sight beneath the waves.

Vex staggered against the railings. His eyes were wild and his arm swung sharply downwards so that Booty squealed as he banged up against the white metal bars.

A voice shouted, 'Stop!'

Vex recovered his feet. He brought the cat back inside the rails as the purser rushed past Malik and stood between the two of them. 'What on earth do you think you're doing to that cat?'

Vex bristled. He threw Booty onto the deck at Malik's feet and Malik scooped the cat into his arms and held him tight.

Angelo Vex pointed at them. 'He . . . that boy . . . he has lost . . . something of mine.'

'Good God, man!' the purser bellowed at him in disbelief. 'Whatever the boy may have done, it does not give you the right to torture a harmless animal.'

Vex collected himself and stood up straight. He adjusted his tie and the purser hesitated, perhaps remembering who he was talking to. Vex turned his back on them and leaned across the railings, transfixed by the waves that washed against the bottom of the hull.

The purser looked between Malik and Vex and back again. He said, 'Do you wish to make a formal complaint against this boy, Mr Vex?'

'What?'

'If you would like to tell me the nature of your complaint . . .'

Vex shook his head. 'It's of no matter.' He waved

them both away as though he was sick of the sight of them. 'A misunderstanding.' He laughed weakly. 'It was a simple misunderstanding. That's all. I apologize.'

The purser touched his beard as he thought it through. He turned to Malik. 'Perhaps you should get some breakfast. We'll be arriving within the hour. You have a long day ahead and it would be good for you to eat.'

Malik didn't go to the canteen for breakfast. He took Booty down to the kitchens and begged a last plate of food from the chef.

'How come your hand's shaking?' asked the chef when he handed him the plate and Malik said, 'I don't know . . . I must be cold,' and he carried the plate below deck with Booty sniffing at the silver foil.

Everyone was still at breakfast and the dormitory was empty. Malik went to his bunk and put Booty down at his feet and the cat rubbed himself against Malik's ankles and purred as though they had never been apart. Malik unwrapped the plate of fish and put it on the floor, just under his bunk, in the usual place. Booty put his head down and began to eat and Malik gave him plenty of space.

He pulled out his rucksack from underneath the bunk, put it on the bed and opened it up. He took out a clean pair of pants, unfolded them and laid them on the mattress. He took out his penknife and opened out the blade, then he found the gaffer tape in the side pocket and pulled at the folded tab till he had a strip the length of his hand. He cut it with his penknife, and stuck the corner of it to the bedpost so it was ready to use.

Then he stepped out of his Wellington boots. He undid the waistband on his trousers, dropped them to the floor and stepped out of them so that he stood in his shirt and underpants. He turned back to the door to check that he was still alone, and once he was certain he put his hand into his pants and brought out Papa's tooth. He turned it once, to see it sparkle, then he stuck it to the top of his left buttock using the strip of gaffer tape.

He stepped out of his pants and tried the clean pair on. The top edge fitted snugly over the small lump. He pulled up his trousers and twisted round to check, with a hand upon his hip. If he wore his shirt untucked, no one would ever know.

Oskar was suspicious. 'How come the cat's back?'

Malik shrugged. He tied Booty's string to the bunk bed. 'Sonny's dad said he couldn't keep him. Anyway, I changed my mind . . .' He stroked down the length of Booty's spine. 'We're going to stick together. If a new family doesn't want my cat, then they can't have me either.'

Oskar's eyes travelled the length of Malik's legs. 'Aren't you going to wear shorts?'

Malik had left his pair out on the bed and he handed them to Oskar. 'You have these. I'm going to stick with long trousers.'

Steffan came in from the bathroom, walking stiffly with long white legs. 'These are a bit too small but they're better than nothing.' He blew his nose and held up his set of keys. 'Look! Miss Price gave me them back.'

The boys were standing by their bunks, packing their things into bags. Alex had nothing but a canvas satchel. When he saw Booty he grinned at Malik. 'I knew you couldn't do it.' He gave Malik the paper-clip ball and told him to keep it.

Miss Price came down with her clipboard and she

called them all together. 'The ship will be docking soon. Is everybody packed and ready to go?' She looked around the dormitory at the gathered boys. 'Good. We shall wait here till I lead you out on deck. Please keep together in lines of two – it's important that I don't lose anyone. Once the ship docks we need to do some checks before we assign you to your families. There will be lots of waiting, so please be patient.'

Already there were people in the corridor, with suitcases in their hands and children holding onto the pockets of their coats. The babble of conversation got louder as the rhythm of the ship's engines changed and Malik felt excited and nervous at the same time. From somewhere above them, the captain sounded the horn.

When Miss Price took them out on deck, the *Samaritan* was still slipping into port, gliding past little fishing boats and large container ships with cargo stacked above the bows in bright bricks of yellow, red and blue. The boys were squashed so tight that Malik shifted Booty up onto his shoulder to keep him safe. He could feel the cat didn't like it. No one liked it. All the faces of the boys were tense.

The captain sounded his horn again as the ship slowed. Malik could feel the floor shudder as the engines strained and the big ship began to turn. Alex was close, pressed tight up against the backs of taller boys. He tugged at Malik's sleeve. 'What can you see?'

Malik stood on tiptoe. He could see buildings on the quayside and tall black cranes like the one back home, with hooks hanging at the end of long chains. He heard the shouts of dockers as they tied the mooring ropes and rolled the gangways into place at the back of the ship. 'Are you all right?' he shouted back to Alex, and the boy smiled nervously. 'I think we have to wait while the first-class get off before us,' Malik told him.

Soon Malik could see passengers walking down the rear gangway. He spotted Mariam and her husband hurry down the steps, where they were met by a chauffeur carrying a placard which must have had their name on it. Malik looked for one that said 'Vex' but he was too far away to make out the letters clearly. He bit his lip, hoping that he would see them leave the ship soon. And then he saw them.

Vex was leading the way in his fur-lined coat and Sonny was held in his mother's arms, looking back at the ship. Malik watched Vex approach a chauffeur in a proper peaked cap, who stood on the dockside in front of a deep red Buick with brightly polished chrome. It wouldn't be long now till they were gone for good. Malik watched their luggage being loaded into the back and saw the chauffeur walk around the car, settling them into their seats and shutting the doors. Finally the car pulled away from the dock.

Malik put a hand round to his back and felt the lump. Vex was really gone. And he still had the diamond.

The orphans were the last to leave the ship. With some of the passengers gone there was more room to move and they stood at the railings to get a glimpse of the city. Directly behind the port Malik saw buildings of old red brick give way to gleaming towers of glass that shone brightly in the sunlight, and at the very back of the city was a range of high hills that were a misty grey in the haze. It wasn't how Malik had imagined.

When it was time for them to leave, Miss Price led them down the steps and across the dock into a large warehouse behind the Port Authority building. The room had a single circular window at one end, about as wide as a bus, and it let in beams of sunlight that showed the motes of dust that floated in the air. A dinner lady got them to queue up and she served them tea from a large urn and apologized that she didn't have biscuits.

Malik didn't normally drink tea, but he drank it now. He went and stood close to Alex who asked him, 'What are you hoping for?'

Malik didn't have to think about it. 'I'd like somewhere nice. Maybe somewhere with a white wooden fence and a garden. How about you?'

Alex shrugged. 'I don't mind. My mum will come and find me as soon as she can and then she'll take me to live with her. So I suppose it doesn't really matter.'

Miss Price came back and asked them to form themselves into lines across the room. A doctor and nurse set up a small table with a cotton screen to shield it from view and they asked the boys to take off their shirts and come behind the screen one by one.

When it was Malik's turn, he got Alex to hold Booty and he went in by himself. The stethoscope felt cold on Malik's skin. He tried hard to breathe normally and when he was asked to cough, he remembered to put a hand across his mouth. The doctor made a note on the form, attached it to a clipboard and passed Malik on to the nurse who looked at the colour of his tongue and parted his hair with a nit comb.

When the doctor had packed up and left, Miss Price called all the boys together. 'Let's form those lines again, boys, just as straight as they were before.' Malik shuffled into position alongside Oskar and Steffan.

'I'm going to ask some families to come in and meet you,' Miss Price continued. 'Please stay in lines and they will pass amongst you. They might ask you questions, so be nice and polite and remember to smile.'

Miss Price gave them each a badge with their name.

Malik looked straight ahead like they did in the army. He heard the chatter of the families as they came through the door, and when he looked down at the floor he saw Steffan's feet next to his own, stepping from side to side. He heard him sneeze loudly, then sneeze again.

Malik held Booty up high so people could see him clearly. He smiled at a couple who walked past and looked at him. They reminded him of Mariam and her husband because they were well-dressed, and although the woman smiled sweetly the man didn't seem very interested. They didn't stop to read his name and Malik thought it was probably for the best.

He could hear Steffan muttering under his breath.

In the row in front, a young couple stopped to speak with Alex. They had a boy with them who might have been their son, and Malik thought he looked only a year or two younger than Alex. Malik watched them smile and nod their heads. He thought they looked just right for Alex.

Another couple walked past Malik without even pausing. Next to him, Steffan was rocking on his heels. He was looking at the floor and talking fast under his breath now. 'She's got brown hair, she's got brown eyes, she has a mole on the side of her neck and a tooth that isn't quite straight. And Dad's got, Dad's got . . .'

Oskar put a hand on Steffan's shoulder. He whispered, 'Steffan, stop it. You'll ruin our chances. What's the matter?'

But Steffan stepped from foot to foot and he

didn't seem to notice. He said, 'Dad's got hairy legs and a hairy chest and he laughs like there's no one else around and I like it when he laughs because I can see all his teeth and I like how big his mouth gets when he's happy.'

Oskar picked up the heavy leather holdall and slung it across his back. He grabbed Steffan by his shirt and led him out toward the door with a hand around his shoulders. 'It's all right, Miss,' he called out. 'I'm taking him to the bathroom.'

Malik watched them go, not sure whether to follow them and perhaps miss meeting his family, so he stayed where he was and the couples passed among the boys and it seemed they talked to everyone but him.

The boys were asked to sit on the warehouse floor while Miss Price took the families to a different room to discuss which of the children they might take home with them.

Everyone was anxious and quiet and Malik was worried about Oskar and Steffan, who still hadn't come back. He watched the double doors at the end of the room but nobody arrived or left. The dinner lady offered them more tea.

Alex sat down next to Malik. 'What do you think? Did you have any luck?'

'I don't think so. How about you?'

'Maybe.'

'I saw that couple who talked to you. The ones with the boy. I liked the look of them.'

Alex nodded. He held his hands in his lap with his fingers crossed.

The double doors swung open and Miss Price took two steps inside and smiled at a boy who wore a green school cap. She held out a hand, 'Come and meet your new family, Christopher.' The boy hurried over with his bag and coat and she led him from the room.

Malik gave Booty to Alex and stood up. 'I'm going to the toilet,' he said. 'I won't be a minute.'

He hurried out into the corridor. A sign showed the toilets with an arrow pointing left and Malik followed it. He turned left again and then right. As he passed one of the doors he looked in through the glass and saw a woman at a desk on a telephone. He went into the toilets and found them empty except for a single locked cubicle. Malik knocked on the door. 'Oskar? Steffan? Is that you?'

A man's voice asked, 'Excuse me?' and Malik said, 'I'm sorry,' and he left the room.

He looked left and right. He didn't want to get lost. He should go back the way he came, but decided instead to go as far as the next corner, and he walked on until he reached a hallway with a staircase. He stood at the bottom of it and looked up through the centre. There must be at least three floors up above, maybe four. They could be anywhere.

Then Malik heard a sneeze. It came from the space beneath the stairs, and he walked around the banisters and bent down to look into the shadow.

Steffan was sitting on Oskar's long leather holdall, blowing his nose. He looked surprised to see Malik. 'What are you doing here?'

Malik crouched under the stairs and crawled up close. 'I was worried. Are you all right?'

'I'm not going with them. I've decided. I don't want a new mother and they wouldn't have us anyway. Not both of us together. We're better off on our own.'

'Where's Oskar?'

'He's finding a way out of here. Do you want to come with us?'

Malik thought about it. 'No. I don't know . . .'

269

There were quick footsteps on the tiled floor and Oskar appeared. 'It works. I found a key that works.' He held a thin flat key separate from the rest on Steffan's ring.

'Malik's coming with us,' said Steffan.

'That's great. It's better to be independent – you'll like it. I found a door that opens out onto the street. There's loads of places out there we can go.' Oskar pulled his bag from under Steffan. 'Come on. Come quick. It's just down here.'

He led them down another a corridor. Malik was thinking quickly. Should he go with them? Or should he stay and chance to luck with a new family? They reached a door. Above it was a window that looked out onto open sky and Oskar put his bag on the floor and slid the key into the lock. 'It takes a bit of wiggling about.' He pursed his lips as though it were unpleasant.

Steffan asked Malik, 'Where's your cat?'

The door clicked open and they could smell fresh air on their faces. Opposite them were shops that were busy. A car drove past. There were people on the pavement going places.

Oskar picked up his holdall and slung it over his shoulder. 'Come on. Quick. Let's go.'

'Are you coming then?' asked Steffan.

Malik shook his head. 'Good luck,' he said.

Steffan stepped outside. 'You too.'

Oskar shook Malik by the shoulder. 'Shut the door behind us.'

The two boys took off across the street, holding their bags tightly as they ran, and Malik saw they had changed back into long trousers. He watched them till they had turned the first corner and disappeared from view and then he closed the door, feeling empty and scared at letting them leave without him, because now he had no one and he might never see them again. He swallowed hard – he had to trust he had made the right choice.

When he returned to the warehouse, Alex still had Booty on his lap. 'Anything happened?' Malik asked him, and Alex shook his head – he had a kind of frozen look on his face. 'You'll be fine,' Malik reassured him. 'I know you will.'

When Miss Price next came to the double doors, she called Malik's name. He shook Alex by the hand, then took hold of his cat, picked up his rucksack and walked across to the double doors. 'Malik,' Miss Price smiled sweetly at him. 'There's someone I'd like you to meet.'

Miss Price led Malik along the corridor, telling him what good fortune it had been. It was a slice of luck that the lady mentioned her love of cats . . . she had arrived late . . . she told them she didn't wish to partake in a parade of children . . . Miss Price walked through a final set of doors and stopped abruptly.

An old lady stood in the centre of the waiting room. She had pale brown skin and narrow eyes. She wore a purple silk blouse with a short string of bright white pearls that nested on her clavicle. When she spoke, her voice was clear and sharp and her accent was unfamiliar to him. 'I am used to cats and exotic birds,' she told him. 'But not young boys. If you choose to live with me, you must be patient whilst I learn.' She had a smile as wide as the harbour, and when she used it, she didn't seem old at all. 'So what do you think, Malik? Will I do?' She waited for his answer, watching him across the top of her spectacles.

Malik said, 'Pardon me, Miss, but I don't think it works like that.'

'Of course it works like that. I can't see any other way it would work. And if we're going to get on, you must call me Lucy.'

Part 3

Lucy Kellaway lived an hour's drive from the port.

Through the windscreen of her car, Malik glimpsed buildings that were impossibly tall and made from glass. The city was much bigger than the town he was used to and it was busy. There were people everywhere – people walking past their car or crossing in front of them at traffic lights, people cycling alongside on quick, light bikes. Malik wound the window down. He could smell cinnamon nuts from a cart at the side of a street and saw a beggar on the pavement rattle a tin for spare coins. He heard a whistle and turned to see a policeman waving at cars from the middle of the street.

Everything was different from home. Everything was new. And it was too big. Too busy. Malik couldn't see how he could possibly live here. He wouldn't even be able to find his way back to the port. He wound up the window and stared down at his knees.

Lucy interrupted his thoughts. 'I go to the the-atre once a week. You can come with me if you like. And we shall eat out in the evenings. I find cooking can be such an ordeal.' She checked her mirror and indicated to turn right. 'We shall have to talk about money as well. What if I give you a small weekly allowance? Would that be all right with you? It would be easier for both of us, I think.'

Malik nodded. He didn't think he could speak.

'Never mind. These things will sort themselves out. Anyway, I always say the best things in life are free.'

Malik waited to see where Lucy lived. He expected to see a white, boarded house with a garden gate and a post box on a pole, but she parked the car in a busy street and pointed up to a third-floor apartment. Beneath it was a gentlemen's outfitters, and across the street Malik saw a bar that had a line of small round tables along the pavement.

'Is this it?' he asked.

Lucy nodded. 'It's not much, but it's home.'

She took him to a double wooden door which had a plate of brass buttons with names written beside them. Inside the door was a large hall. There was an old lift, which ran up through the centre of a wooden staircase; it had a brass grille that you slid across to get in or out.

'I always use the stairs,' Lucy told him. 'It helps to keep me fit.' She started up and Malik followed. 'We're on the third floor. Not too far up but high enough to get some fresh air when we open the windows.'

When they reached the front door, Lucy hesitated. She had the key in her hand. 'How shall we deal with the cats? Shall we just put them in together and see how they get on? I have two Siamese. I expect they'll be fine, but they can be unpredictable.'

Malik hadn't thought whether Booty might find it difficult. He held him close when they stepped inside and her cats came to meet him down the hall. Lucy led the Siamese into the kitchen and closed the door. 'One step at a time might be wise.' She smiled and looked around her. 'Well? What do you think?'

Everywhere Malik looked there was something interesting. He noticed a set of small, carved figures that she kept on a shelf and she had a clock that didn't tell you the time, but told you when the tide would be high or low. On the wall by the door was a framed photograph. Malik looked at it closely and saw a family outside a small house on a beach. There was a mother with a baby in her arms, and a father standing beside a boy who was the height of his waist. There were palm trees in the background. 'That's where I was born,' Lucy told him. 'I came here once on a ship, just like you have.'

'Were you on your own?' asked Malik.

Lucy nodded. 'I'll tell you about it sometime. But not now.'

Malik left his Wellington boots at the front door and followed Lucy down the carpeted hall, past shelves full of books. She showed him into the sitting room. It had a sofa, two upholstered chairs and a harpsichord in the corner. There was also an old gramophone player and a stack of records.

She showed him the bathroom, which had a bath with a shower attached to the taps, so you could choose either one. Malik noted a toilet in the bathroom and another toilet down the hall, and both of them had locks on the door.

Lucy took him to his new bedroom. It was a large room with a big brass bed and maroon wallpaper. He had a writing desk with an anglepoise lamp and a wooden office chair positioned under a window, which looked out onto the bar opposite the apartment. Lucy had left a magazine for him to read.

Next to the brass bed was a chest of drawers and she pulled out the top one to show him it was empty. 'I thought this might do for you.' She looked at his rucksack. 'I didn't realize you would have so little luggage. That was thoughtless of me.' But she smiled her very wide smile. 'We shall have to go shopping once you've settled in.'

Malik didn't want to go shopping, but he said, 'Thank you,' and then he added, 'This is all very nice.'

His stomach had twisted tight, just like it had been at the cottage in the docks, and he thought that it was probably because everything was new, and although it was nice and Lucy was being kind, it wasn't home and this bedroom wasn't his room, and being safe seemed to mean that everything would be painful all over again. He suddenly felt like crying but he held it in.

He put Booty on the bed. 'I'm going to keep him in here with me and let them sniff each other under the door till they're ready to meet.'

'That sounds like a good idea,' said Lucy.

Malik shuffled from one foot to the other.

'Is there something else you need?' asked Lucy.

'Yes, please,' said Malik. 'If you don't mind, I'd like to be alone.'

Malik ran his finger around the room. He touched along the top of the skirting board and up round the frame of the door. He touched the empty shelf and ran his finger along the top of the chest of drawers. He pulled out each of the drawers in turn – they smelled of dust and mothballs. He touched behind the back of the drawers.

His desk had another drawer that was full of sheets of paper and a set of coloured pencils. He turned the anglepoise lamp on and off again, and fingered the catch on the window. The brass bed was hollow when he tapped at the metal frame, so he ran a finger up to one of the brass knobs at the corner of the bed and he tried to pull it off but it wouldn't budge. He tried twisting and the brass knob turned till it fell into his hand. He looked inside the bedpost and saw a bolt that cut across the gap, about half the length of a finger from the top.

Malik reached into the back of his pants and pulled the strip of gaffer tape till he had Papa's tooth in his fingers. This was his most precious possession – the thing that would make Mama smile. He dropped it into the gap and it rattled to a stop against the bolt. He screwed the brass knob back in place.

Booty was scratching at the bottom of the door. Malik went and picked him up and carried him back to the bed. He settled him down on the pillow and tickled him behind his ears, but Booty didn't want to sit still – he jumped off the bed and walked around the room, sniffing where Malik had traced with his finger.

Malik stared at the closed door. He had never felt more alone. He sat at the desk and looked out the window. In the bar opposite there were people talking at a table, leaning close together and laughing. A woman had a tall glass with a bright orange drink and a straw to sip from.

He took a piece of paper, opened the set of coloured pencils and started to sketch his mother's face. He took his time, trying to think about her eyes and her nose, thinking about the shape of her face, but every mark he made was wrong. He had never been able to draw. His face didn't look like Mama at all. It didn't look like anyone. It was just a drawing by a little child, with a scar for a mouth and twigs coming out of her head instead of hair.

Malik used a bright red crayon to put a line through it.

When Lucy knocked at the bedroom door, Malik didn't answer.

She said, 'I thought we should have something to eat.'

Booty sniffed at her feet under the gap in the door.

She said, 'Are you all right in there?'

Malik said, 'I'm not hungry.'

'Perhaps it would be good to get some fresh air?'

Malik didn't answer. After a short while he heard her move away from the door. He could hear her in the kitchen, opening a cupboard door. Running a tap. Scraping the inside of a tin with a fork.

Booty sat watching the bedroom door, waiting for it to open.

After a little while, Malik thought he heard the front door click shut.

He went to the window and waited till Lucy went out of the building. He watched her walk across to the bar and go inside. When she came out, fifteen minutes later, she carried a plate with a stainless steel lid over it. She came back inside the building and Malik heard the front door of the apartment open and then click shut.

Lucy said, 'I'd like to come in. I have some food for you.'

Malik didn't answer.

He heard Lucy put the plate down on the floor.

Booty did a wee on the carpet.

He was over by the door where he'd been scratching to get out. Malik heard it when it was too late and he saw Booty shiver with the shame and indignity as the wet patch spread out across the tufts of oatmeal brown. It went under the door and out into the hall.

When Booty finished, he pawed at the ground to try and cover what he'd done. Malik bent to pick him up but he skittered away under the bed and stayed there.

The room began to smell.

Malik stood a metre from the closed door. He knew he couldn't go on like this – he wasn't being fair either to the cat or to Lucy. He heard her feet on the carpet in the hall, heard her pause outside his room. He opened the door. The wet patch ran under the plate of food with the stainless steel lid. He said, 'I'm sorry,' and he looked at his feet.

Lucy said, 'I thought that cat needed something. Never mind, I'll bring some water.'

She took the plate of food into the kitchen and Malik followed her. She filled a bright yellow plastic bowl with warm water and some soap that smelled of lemon and she handed Malik a sponge. They went back to the bedroom door and she put the bowl on the floor.

Malik saw her wince when she bent on one knee and he said, 'Here, let me. I should do it.' He wet the sponge and scrubbed at the carpet till it smelled better.

When he had finished he looked up. Lucy stood in the middle of the room looking at the pieces of paper on the desk. There were papers on the bed and covering the floor around the window, all of them with faces drawn in coloured pencil, then scrubbed out with red lines through them.

'Who were you drawing?' she asked.

'It's no one,' said Malik.

Lucy walked back into the hall. 'Here's the deal,' she said at the door. 'You get to stay in your room as long as you want. I won't bother you. But you must come across the road and eat with me in the evening.

At seven o'clock. You don't have to talk to me, but you have to eat. We could try it out and see how it goes?'

Malik nodded. 'Would that be all right?'

'If there's a problem, I'll let you know.'

He offered her his hand and they shook on it.

In the hallway, Booty sat back to back with the Siamese, pretending they hadn't met.

'We have a problem with your cat.' Lucy leaned across her plate of grilled mackerel and rhubarb.

'I'm sorry,' said Malik immediately.

But Lucy shook her head, 'There's nothing to be sorry about. He uses the litter tray but he also needs to go out. That's all. He sits on the window ledge and pines. I've only ever had house cats. My Siamese wouldn't know what to do if they were faced with a tree or a bird. And if they ever met a dog . . .' She ate a mouthful of her food, unable to say what might happen if they ever met a dog. She pointed to his supper. 'Don't let yours get cold.'

Malik cut a slice of his chicken escalope and ate it. He put ketchup on his chips.

'It's a question of logistics.' Lucy waved her fork in the air as she talked. 'We live in a third-floor apartment on a busy street.'

'I could take him for a walk,' suggested Malik.

'What a good idea!' Lucy took a sip of her wine. 'Do you know, I think that might work.'

Lucy went to the shops and came back with a blue velvet lead that could clip onto the ring of Booty's collar. She also bought a pocketbook map of the city, marked the street where they lived with a big red dot and turned the corner of the page so Malik could always find it.

Malik planned a route to the park. The most direct route took four streets and it looked easy enough. Booty didn't seem to mind the lead, though he either walked very slowly or very quickly, and sometimes he wouldn't walk at all but would roll on his back in the sun and he wouldn't get up till he was ready. Malik didn't mind. Going slow got him accustomed to the sound of busy streets.

On the way to the park, he passed a barber's shop where he saw a man lying back in a big black chair while his chin was shaved. Further on he saw a sweet shop that had tall glass jars in the window, full of red and yellow sweets. Malik didn't dare to go in. Anyway, he didn't have any money yet.

At the park, Booty dug his claws high into the bark of a tree and stretched himself out. He sniffed at bushes and lay on the lawn with Malik, their heads right next to a big yellow dandelion as they listened to the birdsong.

On the way home, Malik took a different route that he traced on the map with his finger. It took him past a jeweller's shop and Malik stopped and looked in the window at the pretty rings and necklaces. Of all the jewels in the shop, the most expensive were diamonds, and none of the diamonds were as big as the one he had hidden at home. Malik made a point of remembering the price of the ring that cost the most.

At the end of their meal, Lucy left a couple of coins in a dish, as a tip for the waiter.

Malik picked one up. He held it up in front of Lucy's face and flourished his other hand across the front to make it disappear.

Lucy clapped her hands. 'Very good! How did you do that?'

'It's a secret. It's called a French Drop.'

'Fair enough. But it's not over, is it? I want my coin back. I need to pay the waiter for his trouble.'

Malik reached behind her ear. He transferred the coin from his palm to his fingers and made it reappear before her eyes.

'How fantastic. How did you learn that?'

'It takes practice.'

'And do you know any more tricks?'

Malik shook his head. 'I only know that one.'

'Well, it's a good trick to know. Who taught you how to do it?'

Malik wouldn't look at her. He picked up a fork and pushed a green bean around the rim of his plate.

Lucy put the coin back in the little dish. 'I'm sorry. I ask too many questions. People tell me it's a bad habit but I think it's good to be inquisitive. Perhaps you don't agree? I've noticed you never ask me anything.'

Malik put down his fork. 'How much is a ticket for the boat back home?'

'I have no idea but I can find out for you.' Lucy looked worried. 'Don't you like living here?'

Malik shook his head quickly. 'It's not that. I like it very much. But I need to go back, and I can't leave it too long or I'll forget things.'

Lucy laid her hands out on the table. 'Malik, the town where you came from is still very dangerous. It won't always be that way, but at the moment I can't think of anyone that would take you back there. I doubt whether there will even be a ship that goes there.' She hesitated. 'Could I ask why you want to go back?'

Malik watched her carefully. 'People don't always believe me.'

Lucy put her hand on his. 'I will believe you and perhaps I can help.'

Malik made a decision not to tell her about the diamond, but he told her about the soldiers coming to his house and he told her about the dying dog in the cellar and how Papa had tricked him into getting on the ship. And he told her that Mama had disappeared and he didn't know how to find her.

When he was finished Lucy said, 'We can write some letters. That's not difficult. It's all about knowing how to do things and luckily I have some experience.' She pulled her glasses down her nose and gave him a straight look. 'But you should know, Malik, that these things take time. Sometimes they take a very long time and you don't always get the answers you are looking for. You must promise me you won't stop living while you wait.'

Lucy found Malik a school that was close enough for him to walk to. It had small classes and was accustomed to refugees. She bought him a blazer that was too warm and a shirt with a collar that was stiff to begin with, but Malik was pleased they wore long trousers. He made new friends who showed him new games and were impressed that he knew a magic trick to make things disappear. After a little while Malik accepted that the lessons weren't so different from the way he had been taught back home.

Lucy made a point of paying him his allowance on the first day of the week. 'This is for you,' she would say and count out three blue notes and fold them into his hand. 'You can save it or spend it as you wish.'

Malik spent the money the same way each time. He saved one of the notes in the drawer of his desk. He spent another on a bag of fudge from the sweet shop, and he spent the third on a bus ticket down to the port, where he watched the passengers disembark from the tall ships that docked there every Saturday. On the journey he would look out for Steffan and Oskar, thinking he might see them on a street corner somewhere, though he never did.

When the winter changed the weather for the worse, Malik acquired a coat made from sheepskin, a woollen hat and a scarf with the crest of an eagle on it. Lucy often took him to the theatre as she had promised to do and they wrapped up warm, walked back after dark and had a late supper in the bar across the street.

Lucy asked Malik lots of questions about his life before he came to live with her. She asked him Papa's surname, what he did for a living, whether he knew this man or that man, where Mama used to work and what she did for a living. She asked about the name Kusak. Was it common where he came from? Did he know anyone else with a similar name? She asked him the names of the streets in his town, and when he didn't know many of them, she bought a map to work them out. She said there were all sorts of questions that might give them information to help them with their search and Malik didn't mind – he found it a good way to keep from forgetting.

On one such evening, they were in the bar. They had eaten pasta and Lucy had ordered coffee. She put a hand in her bag and produced a large brown envelope that had been folded in half. Malik recognized the stamps on the front.

'I think I have some news of Papa.' She took papers from the envelope and held them out so Malik could see. On the top was a copy of Papa's passport; it had his name, Salvatore Bartholomew, and a photograph that left no doubt.

'That's him!' Malik touched the face with his finger. 'That's Papa! Where did you find him?'

'Malik, I'm sorry but this isn't good news.' Lucy showed him another piece of paper. 'It came with this.' She held out a copy of a certificate of burial, from a graveyard on the outskirts of the town. Malik remembered seeing it on the map they had at home.

Lucy took his hand. When she touched his face, Malik couldn't feel it. 'See the date there? That's about three months after you came to live with me. I think this must be true.'

Malik took his hand away from hers. He put it down under the table and held the front of his trousers. 'What about Mama?' he asked quietly. 'Is there anything there about her?'

Lucy shook her head. 'I've heard nothing of your mother yet. Not a word.'

Malik stayed in his bedroom for a week without coming out.

He heard Lucy ring his school and tell them he was ill.

He heard her clip the lead to Booty's collar and take him for a walk.

He heard her leave plates of food outside the bedroom door.

Later, when Malik decided to come out of his room, he went and stood by the photograph in the hall.

'That's me there,' Lucy told him. 'I'm the little baby in my mother's arms. There's my daddy and my older brother George.'

'You told me you came here in a ship on your own.'

'I did.'

'And did they ever come and find you?'

Lucy smiled sadly. 'No, sweetheart, they never did. That house we are standing in front of was bombed with all of us in it. I don't know *why* it was bombed, but I know *when* and I know by *who*. We weren't very wealthy and my mother had put me in a drawer to sleep and that's where I was discovered. I had to find all this out later, you understand, when I was grown-up. But it's better to know, I think.'

'No, it's not.'

'It will get easier with time. Really, it will.'

'I don't want to know. I mean, if you get a letter about . . . Well, I don't want to know.'

Lucy nodded. 'That's OK. If that's what you want. But don't give up hope, Malik. Don't ever give up hope.'

In the spring there were daffodils on the verges at the side of the busy roads, big banks of yellow flowers. The glass buildings in the city turned pale blue in the mornings and a soft pink in the evenings, just before the sun set.

Malik had a job delivering free newspapers to the houses in the streets around the apartment. He pulled a shopping cart behind him and took the papers out one at a time, folded them and posted them through the letterboxes.

One day it rained while Malik was delivering the newspapers. He had completed only half of the houses when the droplets began to land on his face and he decided to return home. He lifted the canvas lid back over the top of the cart to protect the unde-livered newspapers and he pulled it along behind him as the rain came down heavily and spattered the concrete paving stones where he walked.

At the bar across from Lucy's apartment, the waiters were struggling to pull the awning over the line of tables. Malik waited for the traffic to pause so he could cross the road. On the opposite pavement, a woman in a red dress walked past the window of the gentlemen's outfitters, her head obscured by a black umbrella. She rang the doorbell to Malik's block and stepped inside and Malik saw her hand shake the rain from her umbrella and close it before the door clicked shut.

He stepped out from the kerb, found his way between the stationary cars and pulled the cart up onto the opposite pavement. He let himself into the building using his key which he had hung on a piece of string that was tied to the belt of his trousers. He pulled the cart inside, wheeled it across the stone floor and parked it next to the caged lift, then he pressed the CALL button and waited. He heard the metal gate open and shut on a floor above him before the elevator began to descend, the cables swinging against the edge of the lift shaft with a dull thud.

Malik ran his fingers through his wet hair. If it continued to rain, Lucy wouldn't take them far to eat this evening. Probably they'd visit Giulio's and have pizza at a table by the window. Perhaps they would have a sandwich across the road and Lucy would scowl at the men who stood and smoked at the bar.

He let himself into the flat and hung his coat up on the hook beside the door. As he stepped out of his Wellington boots, Booty brushed up against his ankles, waiting to be fed. He could hear Lucy talking loudly in the living room down the hall and he shouted out, 'Hello', went into the kitchen and took an open can of cat food from the fridge. He forked it out into the three bowls that he lifted from the floor.

'Come in here,' called Lucy. 'Don't worry about the cats for now. Come in here.'

Malik put the bowls down beside the fridge and the cats hurried to sniff at each one, eager to see if there was any difference between them. He walked down the hall and into the living room.

Lucy stood up from her chair and gestured to the armchair opposite. 'There's someone here you will want to see, Malik.'

Malik saw a red dress without flowers and a sweep of blonde hair that was longer than he remembered. The woman stood up. She took a step towards him, holding her arms out nervously, and Malik took the tips of her fingers in his and moved toward her. She was the same as he remembered but different, familiar but changed. The woman put an arm around his shoulders and pulled him close, hugging him tightly, her chin brushing the top of his head. Malik could smell lavender soap on her neck.

'You've grown,' Mama said eventually. She ran her fingers through his hair. 'What have you done to your hair?' she said, and he said, 'I don't know. It's probably the rain,' and she said, 'No. It's not that. It's different.'

Malik stepped back. He saw that she was crying, the kind of crying that makes no noise, the crying that makes your face tremble and run with tears. Malik wanted to see her smile, but his mother kept crying and she stood shaking, one hand held up to her mouth, unable to even speak.

'I'll make us all some tea,' said Lucy.

Malik took Mama's hands from his arms. 'I have something for you,' he told her. 'Wait here. I'll only be a moment.' He ran to his bedroom, unscrewed the bed knob on the bottom left column of his big brass bed and scooped out Papa's tooth with a single finger. The diamond sparkled in his palm as he closed his hand around it.

From the hallway, he could hear Lucy in the kitchen, putting cups and saucers onto a wooden tray, filling the china jug with cold milk from the fridge.

Malik walked back into the sitting room with his hand closed tight. Mama had sat back in the armchair. She dabbed a white cotton handkerchief to the edges of her eyes and Malik reached out and touched her shoulder.

His mother smiled up at him.

It was the most beautiful smile he had ever seen, just for him, better than he remembered or could ever have imagined.

And he hadn't even opened his fingers.

Acknowledgements

Thank you to my agent Sallyanne Sweeney, who has been variously inspiring, patient and hardworking on my behalf.

Thanks to everyone at David Fickling Books, who have taken such good care of me. In particular, Hannah Featherstone and Bella Pearson, who both worked on the text till it sparkled, helping *Close to the Wind* become the book I always intended it to be.

Thank you to David Dean whose artwork looks so splendid on the jacket, and to Sue Cook for her helpful suggestions.

Whilst writing this book I attended courses at New Writing South, tutored by Susannah Waters and Catherine Smith, who both have a gift for knowing what works and are generous enough to share it with the rest of us. Thank you to everyone on those courses who may have commented on my work, particularly Philip Harrison, Sam De Alwis, Roz De-Ath, Stuart Condie, Yvonne Hennessey and Judith Bruce.

And lastly to my family, who make it all worthwhile – to Tanya, for never once saying this was a bad idea; to my lovely boys, Jonah and Nathaniel; to my mum and dad, my sisters Ann and Katie, and to Jessica Smart.

Thank you all.